Blood Sweat & Tears
Essence of Life
A NOVEL BY
LYFE

This novel is a work of fiction. Any references to real people, events, establishments, or locales are intended only to give the fiction a sense of reality and authenticity. Other names, characters, and incidents occurring in the work are either the product of the author's imagination or are used fictitiously, as those fictionalized events and incidents that involve real persons. Any character that happens to share the name of a person who is an acquaintance of the author, past or present, is purely coincidental and is in no way intended to be an actual account involving that person.

ISBN: (13) 978-0-9836039-4-8
Cover design: www.mariondesigns.com
Inside layout: www.mariondesigns.com
Typist: Linda Williams
Editors: Dolly Lopez and Linda Williams

Blood, Sweat & Tears/Lyfe

NEW VISION PUBLICATION

P.O. Box 2815
Stockbridge, GA 30281
www.newvisionpublication.com

First Printing April 2012
Printed in U.S.A.

10 9 8 7 6 5 4 3 2 1

Chapter 1

"Somebody, help! Please, somebody help me!" Kim was screaming at the top of her lungs. What had seemed like a lifetime had just taken less than ten minutes.

The two culprits had entered the house and were in and out. It didn't take long; they had gotten what they came for—ten kilos of cocaine and two hundred thousand dollars in cash—and had left a bloody corpse behind.

As the sirens approached, the neighbors had begun to crowd the streets. The whispers and finger pointing had already started. Everyone knew that Kim and her soon to be husband was selling big time dope, but no one dared to speak on it. Even though he was a bad guy, to the community he was a great man and a great father. Jason would give you the shirt off his back if need be. The elders in the neighborhood were horrified at the news. Jason used to pay off their lawn care, their groceries and repaired anything around the house that needed to be fixed.

In the midst of the action, Kim had not noticed

anything different about her surroundings. Her shirt was covered with blood, sweat, and tears. Everything that they had worked for has gone down the drain.

Miss Gladys, the nosy old neighbor from upstairs, had seen it all and was the one who had called the police. "Kimberley, sweetheart, it's gonna be okay, baby. The police are here now."

Somehow, Jason still had a pulse and his eyes were glued to Kim. With every heartbeat, blood oozed out of his body. Squeezing Kim's hand as tight as he could, she had begun to feel the tension of his grip loosen.

As usual, 911 was a joke. The yells and screams of the crowd didn't even seem to speed the paramedics up. In the 'hood it was always like this. You'd do better trying to drive yourself to the hospital.

"Excuse us! Make a path!" an officer yelled while securing the crime scene off with yellow tape.

The crowd became upset with the untimely actions of the police and paramedics.

Officer Mackey was the first on the scene, asking questions. As usual in the 'hood, no one said or saw anything. Snitching was prohibited.

The guys in the streets that had worked for Jason wouldn't tell the police anything, even if they saw what had happened. Their motto was: *If it happens in the streets, it stays in the streets*. Jason and his crew were governed under their own authoritative administration.

For the few generals and captains that were scattered throughout the crowd watching with inscrutable minds, they secretly swore to avenge their boss. There were no questions asked. There was going to be retaliation of some kind.

"Excuse us, Miss. The paramedics are here. Please let them help the young man."

When Kim looked up, the detective saw the look in her eyes. He knew without a shadow of doubt that whoever the young man lying in her arms was, he was already gone. Detective Carpenter had seen the face of death many times.

Kim's face had begged with mercy just for a few more minutes to be alone with Jason. His hand had slid from hers, and the last few words she heard were, "God, tell my baby girl that Daddy loves her!" Before he choked on his blood, he managed to tell Kim that he loved her. She had felt his pulse stop and knew that he was no longer with her.

Kim had placed her hand over his face and shut his eyes forever, and prayed silently the prayer that she and Jason would say every morning when they would awake: *"My Dearest God in Heaven, today as I journey on this road of success, I ask of you to protect me from my friends. I can handle my enemies. Amen."* As she stood, her knees had buckled at first.

Detective Carpenter had reached his arms out quickly to brace her fall. Walking her to the couch, she began to hit the detective in his chest and started asking him why.

Then, a moment of silence had fallen upon the entire room. With no regard to the blood soaking his shirt, the detective just took her in his arms and tried to comfort her.

With tears in her eyes, she couldn't bear the sight of Jason being put on the stretcher in a black body bag, and wheeled out of their home, never to return.

As she looked in the doorway, Narcotic Agents Mitch Crimson and Thomas Howe had entered. At first her stomach had twitched, but she realized that they were actual police officers that the rest of the force knew.

"Ma'am, I'm with the Narcotics Division. My name is Mitch Crimson, and this is my partner, Thomas Howe.

We don't mean to be rude at a time like this, but in order to help you in any way possible, we would like to ask you a few questions, if that's okay with you."

"Sir, I have no problem answering your questions, but I must inform you that it all happened so quickly. My fiancé, Jason was in the kitchen cooking, and the doorbell rang."

"Ma'am, do you know if he was expecting anybody this evening?"

"I really don't know for sure, because there's always somebody knocking on our door needing to borrow something. I really feel like it's my fault."

"Now darling, why would you say such a thing like that?" Miss Gladys intervened.

"Ma'am, may I ask who you are?"

"Yes, you may. I'm Miss Gladys, Kim's neighbor from upstairs. I've been living here for ten years. I moved here in 1993 after my husband died, and you can say that I've been like the neighborhood watch. But, to tell you the truth, the old neighborhood has disappeared since these young guys that call themselves men have taken over. They are nothing but a bunch of thugs... some young punks. The old people are scared to even walk to the store and walk around the block at night. But enough about that. The matter at hand right now is this young man who was just ambushed and murdered in his own home."

"Ma'am, did you see or hear anything?"

"Yes Sir-ee Bob I did!"

"Ma'am, my name is Mitch Crimson, not Bob."

"Well sonny, excuse my French! But anyway, I was sitting in my window as usual. I don't know where the two men came from, but I could hear the knocks at the door. I could hear Kim asking who was it, but the two gentlemen never responded. That's when I heard Jason's voice. I really can't say what happened next, but the door slammed shut hard. I wasn't sure, so I turned the television down to be nosy, and that's when I heard the first scream. Then, there was silence. Within two or three minutes, I heard gunshots."

"Could you tell us how many gunshots you heard?"

"If you wait, I will. Anyway, as I was saying, I counted as many as I could, but they were so loud and scary that I lost count after seven. Then, silence again, then the door flew open and I saw two huge men come out and dash off into the darkness. It seemed like they had on black boots, Army fatigue pants, a black T-shirt, and a black ski mask like the S.W.A.T. Team wear."

"Thank you, ma'am. Is there anything else you can remember, like a car, their height, their builds?"

"Oh, yes sir. The first one that came looked to be about 6 feet 2 inches and 250 pounds, and his partner about 5 feet 8 inches, and he looked more in shape, weighing about 195 pounds. Now, that's all I can remember."

"Thank you, ma'am. You've been a great deal of help."

The entire time Miss Gladys was running off at her mouth, Detective Carpenter was taking down his personal notes. As Kim got up, she asked Detective Carpenter to stick around after everyone left so she could tell him what really went on in the house. It took about six to seven hours to clean up and for everyone to leave.

It was one of those nights. For it to be September, it was extremely cold outside.

As the last CSI team member was walking out, Kim was so distraught that she could hardly speak. But she had to tell the detective what happened, before the speculations and rumors destroyed her name and the business that she and Jason had built from the ground up. She thought about all the rumors and negativity that was about to hit the streets. "Detective—"

"Kim, please. You can call me Carp."

Detective Carpenter stood 5 feet 9 inches, and was physically fit. He practiced Tae Kwando and did some rock climbing. His dark complexion made him look very intimidating.

"Well Carp, if you don't mind, I'm about to step into the bedroom and change this shirt."

As she made her way through the house, Carp was trying his best to be professional, but the single man in him could not help but watch Kim walk down the hall. The situation was becoming too personal.

Stifling his emotions, he focused his attention on the different things in the house to help him with his investigation, and started thinking about some of the things Miss Gladys had said. Pulling out his notes and going over them thoroughly, his concentration was momentarily distracted by Kim's inner beauty. She didn't do anything but change her shirt, pin her hair up, and wash the blood off of her hands and face. The first impression was a lasting impression in Carp's mind.

Kim stood 5 feet 5 inches, was thicker than all out doors, had a honey glazed brown skin tone, and the cutest face. Carp now knew the meaning of a dime. Her jet-black hair had made the total package a complete one.

When she stopped at the end of the hallway to enter the living room, he had to get a hold of his thoughts. *Damn! What am I thinking about? This woman has just lost her husband right in their home, and then on top of that, he died in her arms. What kind of a man am I? I'm sitting here being a perverted jerk while this woman is grieving!*

"Carp, would you like something to drink... coffee or tea?"

He really wanted to say no and get up and leave.

The bulge in his pants had started to rise, but the man in him—the homicide detective in him—made him say yes. A few more minutes with her alone under different circumstances, Carp knew that he would have had her sprawled out on the kitchen table.

After regaining his thoughts and composure, he was ready to begin his homicide detective work. The game of Twenty Questions was about to begin. But before he could open his mouth and get the first question out, Kim had already begun to spill her guts.

"Carp, I really don't know where to begin, but I will be 100% honest with you. Off the record though, Jason sold coke. I don't want to start off by lying. Now that's off my chest, I feel a little better. Anything else you can record."

As Carp pulled his pen and pad out, she had gone into detail from beginning to end, trying not to leave anything out. He knew she was strong.

She had begun to explain what happened that night, but paused just for a second. But after making eye contact with Carp she didn't hold anything back. "Carp, it happened so quickly. I heard the knock on the door. When I asked who it was, no one answered. At first I really didn't pay it any attention, and by the time I got up off the couch Jason was coming out of the kitchen. He asked me if there was a knock at the door. By the time I responded to his question, he was already heading for the door. He was so sure of himself and confident about our security and wellbeing that he never asked who was at the door. He always just opened it. When he reached the door and unlocked it, it burst wide open."

"Kim, at that point what happened?"

"Jason had fallen backwards and I started to scream, but my scream was cut short by the two big guys coming through the doorway. I really didn't know what was happening at first."

"What would make you say a thing like that? Didn't you know at that instant y'all were about to be robbed?"

"Well, when they busted in, I thought we were being robbed. Then my eyes focused and I heard their voices. They sounded like cops, so I thought we were being busted."

"What would make you think that?"

"They had their guns drawn. The first one had a Tech-9 or Uzi. The other one had two Glock 40's. Their T-shirts had D.E.A. in bold white letters."

"Is there anything else you can remember?"

"No, that's about it. Wait! Wait! Carp, there is something else. They both had badges hanging from a chain, like the one that dog tags are on... something like the one you're wearing!"

Carp froze instantly, shocked at her accusation. He couldn't believe that the two robbers were actually dressed like undercover cops.

She continued describing how they came in. They screamed that they were the police and made her lie down with her face in the carpet. This had Carp puzzled. "Then, I heard one of them speaking to Jason, asking him where the dope was. With my face down in the carpet and fearing for my life, I could barely hear Jason's voice as he tried his best not to give the location of the dope or safe."

"Then, there was a loud slapping sound. I could only imagine what had happened to Jason. The loud smack was the butt of a gun slapping his face. His scream brought about sudden terror in my thoughts. The bigger of the two men suddenly snatched Jason to his feet, while the smaller one put one of the Glock 40's to my head. No words could define the fear that I was going through. When Jason wiped the blood from the side of his face and saw me with the gun pressed into my skull and the tears running down my face, he didn't even think twice about telling them that the safe was in the kitchen under the sink…"

…Being directed into the kitchen, Jason didn't even hesitate about opening the safe. He had been on enough robberies himself growing up in the 'hood to know that these two individuals were not playing any games. They were about their business. When he finally finished entering the last digits into the keypad, the bottom shelf of the cabinet slid out from under the sink. When he turned around, the big man was handing him a black duffel bag. Everything was happening so fast. All he could do was think about Kim.

When the secret compartment opened, Jason saw the Desert Eagle, but thought twice because of the second man. He knew in his mind that if he gave them all the dope, he could holla back at his connect and be straightened out later, and more than likely he would put a bounty on their heads. Leaving the gun in its place, he decided to cooperate and put the bricks in the bag.

When he had put the last one in the bag, he thought that the position that the robber was standing in and because of his height, he really couldn't see all the way under the cabinet. Turning to hand the bag over was the last action that Jason would ever do.

Before he could blink, his eyes had locked with the big guy. The look in his eyes had informed Jason that he should have went on and just gave up the money too. But, it was too late. The rapid fire had shattered the dishes as he fell. Jason had been gunned down instantly…

"'Stupid! All you had to do was give me the money and you would've lived, you stupid piece of shit!' is what I heard the gunman say," Kim said, and continued…

The big man had to finish the job. He bent over and

cleaned out the safe himself, even grabbing the gun. Not wasting any time, he turned and ran out of the kitchen, headed down the hallway and entered the living room. "Come on! Let's get the fuck out of here!"

"What about her?"

"Damn her! Let's go!"

"Tonight is your lucky night. I told you that you might live. But I'm sorry about your man."

Kim had never looked up, but the words had felt like a knife in her side.

The door was wide open as the second man made his way out, never looking back. The two had dashed into the darkness and vanished.

Even though it had seemed like an eternity, Kim still lay face down, not sure whether they were gone or not.

Then, the yells from the hallway had given her a boost of energy and some strength to get up. Not caring about anything or anyone, her main concern was getting to Jason.

She rounded the couch and froze in her tracks when she saw Jason crawling down the hallway with all his strength. Snapping back to reality, she ran to help him. Not realizing how many times he had been shot, she just helped him to his feet and guided him to the living room where he finally collapsed. She knew he was a very strong individual, and the only reason he was still alive was due to pure adrenaline and his willpower to live...

"Carp, that's when I realized the seriousness of the situation and I started to cry. My yells, screams and pleas for help were answered by Miss Gladys."

As she was finishing up her statement, Carp had finished jotting the last details down, and he was wondering about a few things. He thought for a second and decided that any further questions he had could wait for a later date. The woman had been through a terrible ordeal. He really didn't know how she was able to hold herself together the way that she was. He knew that the average person, after having gone through an experience such as this one, would have had a nervous breakdown by now.

Carp's thoughts were interrupted by a knock at the door. "Are you expecting anyone?" he asked.

"No, not this early in the morning... unless my mother has heard and came over to check on me."

"Did you call and inform her?"

"No, I haven't had the chance, now that I think about it."

Carp was not about to take any chances on the robbers coming back to finish the job. As they made their way down the hallway, Carp had his Glock 40 out and had already put one in the chamber. "Who is it?" he asked.

"Kane!" a deep voice came from the other side of the door.

"Carp, he's okay. He's a friend of the family."

As Carp holstered his weapon, the door came open and all he saw was a mountain of a man towering over the two smaller ones in front of him.

Chapter 2

"Cash, wake up boy! Your phone hasn't stopped ringing since we went to sleep last night. You need to answer it. I know it's one of them little nasty hoes you be messing with!"

"Damn, Kwantie! If you want to know who it is, you answer it!"

"Okay then, Mr. Smart Ass. Hello! Who the fuck is this?"

"Good morning to you, Kwantie. I didn't mean to disturb you this early, but I need to speak to Cash. It's urgent. Tell him it's about our little brother, Jason."

"He's in bed. What is it?"

"Bitch, put my brother on the got-damn phone!"

"Cash, here. Get the phone. Your brother said it was urgent."

"Yo, what's up?"

"Man, why the hell you ain't been answering your phone? Anyway, while you was over there fucking that dumb ass broad, Jason was gunned down and robbed at his house."

"Is he a'ight?"

"Hell no, nigga! He's gone! Get your ass up and meet me at Kim's!"

Pulling into the driveway, Cash noticed his brother and his right-hand man sitting in his black Suburban. But something was strange. There was a green Crown Vic parked in the driveway also. Noticing the yellow caution tape in front of the house made Cash a little nervous, but he knew he had to face reality. Being the oldest of the three, he had to get a grip on himself.

Tapping on the window of the black truck, his brother opened the door and climbed out with tears in his eyes.

"Lil' bro, you a'ight? Man, are you up to this?"

"Man, they killed Jason, and we haven't heard nothing from Kim. P-Nut had heard early this morning from Big Country, and called me."

"Word? Well, whose fucking car is this right here?"

"I don't know, but it looks like one of them D.T.'s. You strapped?"

"You know it! If this bitch got a nigga in there, I'll murder both of them!"

As Kane and Cash made their way up the driveway with the two bodyguards and guns drawn, they were ready to cause bodily harm to anyone in the house that didn't belong. Kane knocked on the door.

"Who is it?"

"Kane."

When Kim opened the door she could see Kane towering over the two bodyguards, and she cracked somewhat of a smile. As her eyes locked on their guns, she hurried and broke the tension, noticing Cash's eyes were looking past her. "Detective Carpenter, it's okay. This is my brother-in-law."

"Hello guys. I'm sorry to have to meet you in this situation. I'm Detective Carpenter, but you can call me Carp. I've been assigned to this case. Kim here was filling me in on all the details of what happened. I know y'all probably want to handle this y'alls' way, but please give us a chance before y'all intervene. I can't promise anything, but I will give a hundred and ten percent to solve this case. This isn't the first attack. To be honest, Jason was on our list of high profile cases. There were a couple of other guys that we had our eyes on, and all of a sudden they came up missing."

"Well, Carp, we can't promise you nothing, but if you don't have any information within two weeks, we will intervene."

"I respect that guys, but if you get in my way, then you will become part of the case and I'll have to arrest you too... haul y'alls' asses downtown and take you through all those dumb ass procedures."

"Well, Carp, you got two weeks. Now, get the fuck out of my brother's house, pig!"

"Kane—that's what they call you, right? It takes respect to get respect, so I'll leave because of the way you conducted yourself. But your brother, Cash better watch how he talks to me. I could make your life hard, trust me!" Walking out the door, Carp looked back and nodded. "Oh yeah, guys. Good luck. Cash, as for you, I'll catch you later."

As Carp made his way down the walkway, he turned just in time to catch Cash pointing his fingers at him like he was holding a gun. But Cash noticed Carp pointing his finger from the side of his waist.

"Kim, what the fuck happened, and what did you tell that pig?"

"Cash, fall back, son!"

"I'm saying, she didn't even call us, bro. We had to find out from da streets."

"Kane, I'm sorry I didn't call, but it all happened so fast, and the police were everywhere. As you can see, Detective Carpenter stayed all morning. I haven't even called my mother. Plus, I didn't want y'all seen by these pigs. Jason had already explained to me what to say if the police ever came. And Cash, as far as you, you better stop disrespecting me! You wouldn't do it if Jason was standing here, so don't start now. I am still part of this family. I'm your sister-in-law whether you like it or not."

"My bad, Kim! You know how I be. Please accept my apology baby girl."

"Accepted, boy."

As Kim sat down and explained every detail to them, Kane was trying to put everything in his mind together, while Cash was thinking revenge.

"Kim, pack some clothes and go out to your mother's house for a while. It's about to get hectic out here."

"Kane, I'm not going anywhere. This is my house. I'm not running or hiding. I'm just as gangsta as y'all are. Why do you think Jason was with me for so long? We were a modern day 'Bonnie and Clyde'. Even though they took him away from me, that doesn't stop what we had going on. Kane, every deal that he made I was there, so everyone knows me, and sometimes I had to make deals by myself, so I know how to handle myself out there in the streets. Anyway, who else are you gonna trust to move what we were moving?"

"Kim, you're right. Jason always told me that you

were a gangsta ass bitch—I mean that in a good way. But this is my operation, and everything goes the way I say. First, we're gonna get past the mourning and his funeral. After we handle all of that, then we'll handle business. But as for now, nobody on this team will be moving anything. This week is dedicated to Jason. So, make your calls and let your people know that everything will be back to normal next week."

"Kane, you letting her take over Jason's shit?"

"What part didn't you hear me say, Cash? That's what the nigga wanted. As a matter of fact, you need to be focused on what the fuck is going on out there in the streets. Take Nut and Country with you and come up with something; who just bought a new car, who's trying to get rid of some work for the low-low… anything out of the ordinary. Kim, you're coming with me."

"Where we going?"

"First rule Kim, never question me. You are family, and as long as I'm alive, no harm will come to you and I will never bring it to you. My brother loved you to death, and now that he's gone, I will!"

"Welcome to Better Aiming Shooting Gallery. Please enter your four digit code and secret voice password."

"Kim, have you ever shot a gun?"

"I'm not about to answer that."

"Jason said that you drive a hard bargain. At least I don't have to worry about you telling nothing, like them snitch ass niggas around me."

"Kane, if you know they're snitching, why do you have them around you?"

"Let's just say they won't be telling on me. The one

thing you will learn will be that I keep me an insurance policy."

"Mr. Woodson, entry has been granted. Are you going to the gun range or to the warehouse?"

"Gun range, and I have a guest."

"Thank you Sir. What guns would you like today?"

"For starters, bring me a 380, a couple of Glocks, and something with firepower."

Kim was surprised. She knew Jason said that they went to the gun range, but she didn't know that it was of this caliber.

After hours of target practice, Kim became acquainted with the Glock 40. The way she handled it, Kane was impressed. Every target she aimed at was hit at center mass and a couple of head shots. She was a born killer and didn't even know it, but by the time Kane would finish with her, she would be ready to join the Navy Seals.

Kane and everybody around him had gun permits, and it was mandatory that each member spend five hours a week at the range.

The streets were about to see a different side of the Woodson boys. Right now there were no clues, but Kane remembered Carp saying that there were two other bodies that were never found. With a smile to his thoughts, Kane knew that there were about to be a lot more bodies coming up missing.

Staring at Kim as she fired the last of the rounds in her magazine, he could see why his brother was in love with her.

Chapter 3

"People, as we come together today to wish Brother Jason Woodson a farewell, let this be a sign that no matter what you're doing, good or bad, when your Higher Power calls, ain't no timeouts or hold on's. It's your time. All you can hope for is that you're right with Him. Before we close and proceed to the burial place, his wife, Kimberly Woodson would like to read a poem entitled 'Your Spirit'."

"I know that no matter what,
You will always be with me.
When life separates us,
I'll know it is only your soul saying goodbye to your body,
But your spirit will be with me always.
When I see a bird chirping,
I will know it is you assuring me you are free from pain.
When the fragrance of a flower catches my attention,
I'll know it is you reminding me,
To appreciate the simple things in life.

When the sun shines through my window and awakens me,
I'll feel the warmth of your love.
And most of all, when I hear the rain drops patter
Against my window sill,
I'll hear your words of wisdom
And will remember what you taught me."

"I love and will miss you, baby!"

"Now, that was a nice piece, Sister Woodson. He will be missed greatly in this community, and we will always love Jason. We have another poem reading by Cashmere Woodson."

"Good afternoon, church. Me and Jason go way back. We were more than cousins. When him and Kane took me in after my parents went home, we have been like the 'Three Amigos'. I don't have any brothers from my parents, but they are my brothers from another mother."

"On my way here today, I didn't know what I was going to say, so I asked myself, 'What would Jason say if he was here?' Then, I heard his voice, and he told me that he was here. He laid on my heart these words for everyone:"

"When your day starts tomorrow without me,
Please try to understand,
That an angel came and called my name,
And took me by the hand.
The angel said my place was ready in Heaven far above,
And that I had to leave behind,
All those that I truly and dearly loved.
But, when I walked through Heaven's gates,
I felt so much at home.
For God looked down, smiled at me,
And told me, 'Welcome home'.
So when tomorrow starts without me,

Don't think I'm far apart.
For every time you think of me,
I'm right there in your heart."

"Love you, cuzzo!"

"Thank you, Cashmere. That was beautiful. Just know, people, that when tomorrow starts, it doesn't start without your loved one. Brother Jason and Brother Cashmere lost their parents together and overcame their problems. Now, Brother Jason has gone home to be with his parents to make a place for us."

"Now, as we get ready to make our way to the burial site, I ask everyone to drive safely and stay close to each other. We will not have a police escort. Please stand."

"Excuse me, church. Please forgive me. I have something to say."

"Brother Kane Woodson, please come up."

"Church, please forgive my rudeness. I wasn't gonna say anything because my brother from another mother had spoken, and Jason's wife, Kim, as far as I'm concerned, had delivered some special words. But Jason had laid his hand on my heart too. He said he's free now. He said:"

"Don't grieve for me.
God took my hand when I heard Him call.
I turned my back and left it all.
I couldn't stay another day,
To laugh, to love, to work or play.
Tasks that are left undone must stay that way.
I have found that peace at the close of day.
If my parting has left a void,
Then fill it with remembered joy.
A friendship shared, a laugh, a kiss,
These things I too will miss.
Be not burdened with times of sorrow.

I wish you the sunshine of tomorrow.
My life has been full, I savored much;
Good friends, good times, a loved one's touch.
Perhaps my time seemed all too brief;
Don't lengthen it now with undue grief.
Lift up your hearts and share with me,
God wanted me now… He set me free."

"Love you, lil' bro! I want to thank everyone for coming out. As we put my brother in the ground, please don't shed a tear of pain. Please make them tears of joy."

Chapter 4

"Cash, wake up, baby. Your phone is ringing."

"Who dis?"

"Shut the fuck up, nigga! What we did to your brother was nothing compared to what we are going to do to you!"

"*What?* Who dis? You know who you fucking with?"

Before he could finish his words, a loud explosion came from outside his house. Grabbing Kwantie and diving to the floor saved their lives. The blast shattered the entire neighborhood. The windows exploded from the heat of the fire ball.

"Kwantie, stay down and call Kane! Tell him everything!"

"Where you going, baby?"

The look in his eyes told her everything. "I love you, Kwantie! That's all you need to know, baby. But niggas done fucked up when they brought it to the house."

Crawling on the floor through the house, he reached the hallway closet just as the back door had come off of its hinges. Before rolling into the walk-in closet, he grabbed a piece of a broken mirror. He slid the wall back and grabbed his vest and two fifty cals. He didn't know how many were out there, so he loaded his favorite toy; his M-16 with the grenade launcher. Cash was a real animal, and they had just awakened a demon.

Using the piece of the mirror to peek around the corner, he tried to anticipate the intruders' next move. A few seconds had passed before he noticed movement coming down the hallway. He counted six guys. Thinking to himself, he became even more upset with the situation. *Who da fuck do they think I am? Six guys! That's all? I'ma show these motherfuckers they better send an army at me the next time! They won't catch me slipping like Jay!*

As the fourth man entered the hallway, the first two were damn near standing in front of him at the entrance of the closet. Moving as slowly and quietly as he possibly could, he raised the two fifty cals and put one to the back of the man's skull and squeezed. Before anyone could react they were trapped, not knowing which way to run.

The sound of the skull exploding had startled the second man as the fragments covered his face. By the time he wiped his face one time, Cash had burst out of the closet and put three in his chest and one in his face.

The last two fired as many rounds as they could, not knowing what they were hitting or shooting at.

Cash dove to the floor before the second body could hit the ground, letting off shots simultaneously. He was shooting at what he thought were two more bodies. Two had turned to one, but he wasn't sure. The last two men had never made it down the hall, and the other two at the end turned and ran out. Cash was not about to move until he saw movement. As he laid there in darkness, he hoped that Kwantie stayed where she was.

A few hours had passed and the sun was coming up. The blood from the body nearest him had soaked into his carpet.

"Cash, you straight?"

"Who dat?"

"Nut and County!"

"Where's Kane at?"

"Outside in the truck. He told us to come in first. Kwantie called us. Are y'all okay?"

"Yeah. Let me see y'alls' hands. Matter of fact, tell Kane to come in." As he got up, he ran to the bedroom to find Kwantie where he left her with his Glock. "Baby, I'm sorry. Are you okay?"

"Yes. Cash, were you hit? What's going on, baby? They came in our house, Cash! You said this wouldn't happen!"

"Baby, chill out! I'm gonna take care of this, I promise. But for now, I have to get you out of here. Pack some things."

"Where are we going?"

"*We* ain't going nowhere, but you're going to your mother's for now until I find out what the fuck is going on."

After she packed her things, Cash grabbed her bags and made his way down the hallway, stepping over the dead men's bodies.

"Cash, they're dead! You killed them?"

"Close your mouth and your eyes and come on. Nothing happened. You didn't see or hear nothing. You've been at your mother's for two weeks. We had a bad argument, I slapped you and you couldn't take it no more."

When they got to the front door, Nut and Country grabbed her suitcases out of his hands as he stared at

Kane getting out of the truck and opening the door for Kim. "Nut, do me a favor. Here's five grand. Get her to the airport, put her on the first plane to JFK and give her the rest. Big dawg, make sure she gets her ass on that plane to New York."

"A'ight. Soon as she's on the plane I'll hit you."

"Big Country, help me with these bodies."

Looking over his shoulder, he watched Kwantie get in the car. With tears running down her face, she blew him a kiss. Blowing one back, she knew he loved her.

"Lil' bro, what da fuck is going on here?" Country asked him.

"Man, my phone rang early this morning. Some nigga had said some slick shit about I'm next, then my car blew up. By the time I made it to the closet, six muthafuckers were in here."

"Well, why do I only see two bodies? I thought you knew how to shoot, lil' nigga."

"Evidently I do. I'm still here. I domed the first one, hit the second one up, but something strange happened. The last two never came all the way in, and the other two turned and hauled ass. I don't have no neighbors, so I don't know where the hell they vanished to."

"We'll get everything out and set the house on fire. You won't be coming back here no more."

"What's up with you and Kim?"

"Fuck you mean? She was on the way to help me murder something."

The look Cash gave Kane let him know that he didn't believe him. The family was falling apart, and Kane hoped that it wasn't over any pussy. Kane couldn't figure out what it was about Cash and Kim, but Cash didn't like her as much as he portrayed.

"What's up, Kim?" Cash asked her.

"You. What's poppin', bro?"

"Shit, these niggas are trying to kill something that won't die."

"Cash, you want me to set the house on fire with the bodies in it, or take them to our people?" Country asked.

"Big Country, man, right now we don't need no fuck up's. Two bodies in my house that don't belong there will start a hell of an investigation. So, do what you do best."

"Hello. Who dis?"

"That bird just took off and it will land in two hours."

"Right. I appreciate that. Your girl said she needs two packs of ground beef from JB's Butcher Shop."

"Gotcha. Tell her I'll be home in two hours and don't start without me."

"Yo, when you get there tell Mr. JB that we will be doing bizness a lot over the next couple of days."

"Peace!"

Chapter 5

When the truck pulled up to the back of the butcher shop, JB was already in the back with the loading dock secured. If there was anyone they could trust outside of the family, it was JB.

Kane and JB had met in prison. They both had something in common. They were real standup guys. One day while talking, JB explained that he wanted to be connected. Kane asked him if he could run a butcher shop. JB laughed until he saw that Kane was serious. Then the two exchanged information.

Kane was home a few years before he was finally contacted by JB. His first week home, JB had run into some niggas he had clapped up. They almost caught him slipping, but Kane had Nut and Country pick him up from prison and they hung out with him the first week.

As JB stepped out of the truck, Nut saw some movement in his rearview mirror. Upon informing Country, they pulled out of JB's driveway and turned the corner.

As JB fondled his keys, he heard a car door open and three dudes got out. Trying to hurry, he dropped his keys. The first man out of the car started shooting. JB dove into the bushes and ran for his life. The other two took off after him as the first man ran back to get the car.

More shots rang out. JB was already jumping the fence in his backyard. As he made it to the second fence, the two men let off a couple of more shots. When JB fell off the fence they thought they had hit him. Just like a lion, they could smell and taste his blood.

As JB got up to run, he felt a pair of massive arms lock around his neck. Nut was in front of him with his finger over his lips telling him to be quiet. Once JB realized who it was, he calmed down, and Big Country released him and gave him a pistol.

In a blind spot of the alley, the two men came over the fence. As soon as their feet landed, they came right back off of them. JB handled his business alone. He stepped right out of the bushes to let the two men see his face.

Nut and Country smiled at each other as they watched the young man put in work. Before the bodies hit the ground, Nut and Country were dragging them to the truck.

JB wasn't finished. He gave Nut the gun back and asked Country for his. At first Country didn't know what to say until JB explained that there were three men. No sooner than Country handed him the gun, they heard a car door slam and footsteps coming closer. When the man made his way down the alley, JB was standing back in the bushes.

The man's eyes weren't adjusted to the darkness yet, because if they were he would have seen death coming. JB stepped out and smashed the back of the gun into the man's skull. The dude dropped his gun and collapsed to the ground unconscious.

Nut said, "Don't kill him yet. We got something special for his ass."

After they tied him up and put duct tape around his mouth, they loaded him into the truck.

JB knew there was no escaping the streets now. He felt that he would always owe Kane, Nut and Big Country for saving his life.

Pulling out of the neighborhood, they needed to fill the tank up. Nut hated driving his new Excursion, but for the work they were doing it always came in handy. Just like any man with a new toy, he named his Excursion "Tsunami" because of the amount of bodies it would haul all over the State of South Carolina.

Pulling up to the Texaco gas station, he noticed a police cruiser across the street at the Sweet Tooth Cafe. Country went in and paid for everything, while Nut kept his eyes on the cruiser. Pulling out of the gas station and heading for the highway, all three men watched as the cruiser pulled off right behind them. It wasn't a quarter of a mile before the blue light came on.

Nut pulled over with the quickness. As the officer exited the cruiser, his hand was already on his gun.

"Excuse me Sir. How are you doing tonight?" the officer asked.

"Fine, officer. May I ask what the problem is?"

"You did not use your signal coming out into traffic. May I see your license and registration, please?"

"Shots fired! Shots fired! All officers in the vicinity of Whitner and Osborne respond immediately with caution!" the radio attached to the officer's collar suddenly blared.

"Well, guys, it's your lucky night. Here's your license and registration. Drive carefully!"

"What's up, Kane?"

"Nothing, JB. Got some more work for you, man. These two dummies tried to kill Cash."

"Oh yeah? Well, you know how I do. How are those big ass dogs doing?"

"Hungry as hell, and they're not dogs. They're Bull Mastiffs, and they are eating me out of house and home. My girl is about to have a litter. If you want one, let me know. Nut, you and Country drag them to the cleaning room. Cash and I will be there in a minute."

"Kane, I don't mind working for y'all, but when have you started bringing bitches around?" JB asked.

"Well JB, you know how we consider you family? She is also family. And that's what we have to talk to you about."

"Well, don't be shy. Spit it out."

"Kim, come here. Kim, this is JB. He's been with the family for the last four years. What we're about to show you may make you throw up, but understand, this is why we have lasted so long in the game."

"JB, nice to meet you."

"The same to you."

"Slow down, dawg! This is Jason's wife, and she's gonna pick up where he left off. Oh yeah. What's up with your cousin?"

"Who, that nigga, E-Dubb?"

"Yeah. Tell him I need some info. Whatever the price is, we got him. Do he still own bouncers? As a matter of fact, after we finish this shit we need to pay him a visit."

"Well guys and girl, let's go inside. Kim, once again, my shop is yours. All I ask of you is to call in advance. It makes it a lot easier. My shop is at your disposal."

Making their way to the cleaning room, JB handed everyone a long white trench like coat and a pair of goggles. Once everyone entered the room, he locked the door from the inside.

Nut and Country had already stripped the men down and tied their feet to the hooks on the meat racks.

"Hold on, guys. Did you get their prints and their pictures?"

"Yes, JB. We're waiting on you to do your part."

"Well, hold them up. Cash, hand me that drill."

While JB drilled into the top of the first man's skull, Kim didn't stop watching. Inside she had become cold. If these guys had anything to do with Jason's death, she would take the drill and do it herself. So, watching didn't bother her like everyone thought it would.

Cash watched her closely as she begin to smile as the blood poured down the drain. Once the drops slowed, he put the bodies onto a conveyor belt and pressed the start button.

Not knowing what was about to happen next, the teeth on the grinder started turning, and Kim watched the bodies being mutilated. As the teeth ground and churned, the remains filled up 50 pound ground beef bags. Once the last bag was full, Nut loaded them all into the truck, and Country helped JB and Cash spray the place down.

"Well, lady and gentlemen, it was nice doing business with you today, and I hope to see you soon. Kane, don't forget about one of those pups when they're ready."

"Gotcha, homie. Let me holla at you for a second. JB, my family has been targeted by some unknown crew, so keep your ears to the streets and your eyes open."

"Man, as soon as I hear a squeak, I'll hit you up. What's up with Cash? He seems a little different, man."

"He's a'ight. He had to burn his house down and send his piece of pussy back home 'til we find out what's going on. Before I forget, we got to hang out this weekend. We need to speak to Ewing and get him to run those prints and get me any information he can. Anything is something right now."

"I'm on it Kane, be easy cuz."

"See ya Friday, unless something pops up. It's seven grand in your car."

Chapter 6

Riding past JB's Butcher Shop, the two undercover agents, Thomas Howe and Mitch Crimson, noticed Kane's truck parked in the rear. At first Mitch was going to keep driving by, but the look on his partner's face told him that they should pull into the parking lot. Sitting outside and staking out criminals had become part of their everyday ritual. Hours would pass by before they moved on. Mitch did all of the driving while Thomas always got out and did all of the police work.

Times were getting hard for these two. They had been on the force since the early nineties. Money was good to them back then. The hustlers from the early crack era had no problem paying their "street taxes", but this new generation of hustlers were not trying to hear or pay them anything.

Mitch and Thomas were living outside of their means, and people on the force had started talking.

The police force was falling apart. No one trusted

anyone. With a new detective snooping around and trying to be on every scene, they knew they had to hit one major lick and get the hell out of Dodge.

"Hey Mitch, what do you think they're in there doing? Do you think this is one of Kane's stash houses?"

"Well, ain't no telling. That black muthafucka has his shit together. He hasn't gotten caught yet, and there's no one that will tell on his ass."

"I feel you, partner, but you know just like I do that where there's a will, there's a way. Trust me, partner, we'll find the needle in that haystack. If it's the last thing I do, them Woodson boys will be in jail or dead."

"Thomas, you're gonna let this shit stress you out to the point that you won't be able to enjoy the money we're gonna get from their asses."

"Yeah, you're right, Mitch. The ball is already rolling and the wheels have been set in motion. When we finish, we will be able to retire, and fuck a pension!"

"But, we have only one problem, Thomas. Those assholes didn't handle their business. Cash is still alive."

"I knew we should have gone in first. Those rookies can't ever do shit right."

"Yeah. I don't know what the fuck they were thinking about, but that black ass nigga, Cash must have a rabbit's foot up his ass, 'cause they didn't even graze him."

"A rabbit's foot my ass, Mitch! God almighty Himself was in that house with him. He has to have nine lives, and if he does, I'm gonna try my damndest to use each one of them up!"

"Well, at least we don't have to worry about Jason anymore. That was probably one of the easiest jobs we've done."

"Yeah, partner. I must agree. But did you see the look on that bitch's face when we came through that door?"

"Thomas, watch your mouth, man! You know I love that pretty ass bitch!"

"My bad, Mitch. But tell me something. It's okay for you to call her a bitch and not me?"

"You damn right! That's *my* bitch. That's why."

While sitting in the car arguing, Thomas noticed Cash come out of the back door by himself. As Mitch started the ignition, he waited before following Cash to make sure that he didn't have any stragglers. The two agents knew that with the loss of Jason and the attempt on Cash's life, Kane and Cash would beef their security level to its highest. There was no time to call for backup. They pulled out of JB's parking lot, trying to look as inconspicuous as possible.

Cash's mind was so stuck on revenge that he didn't even notice that he was being tailed. He was a man on a mission.

Cruising down North Main Street, the Anderson City Police Department building was still under construction as he pulled up to the intersection. The traffic light had caught him and turned red. Looking from side to side, he noticed that the diner where all the police ate was empty. Then, he looked at the gym that sat directly across from the diner and saw the "Closed for Renovation" sign in the windowpane of the front door.

A construction worker that was directing traffic had failed to get Cash's attention so that he could turn down the side street.

As Cash waited for the light to turn green, he was so deep in thought that he didn't even notice the two agents about four car lengths behind him, and the construction worker that had walked up to his car and tapped on the passenger side window.

Cash's deep thoughts were interrupted so quickly that

he was startled. He reached under the seat and grabbed for his gun. With a blunt still in his mouth and gun cocked, he let the tinted widow of his Benz down slowly. "Aye yo! Can I help you, man? You're tapping on my window like you know me or something, playboy!"

"No, *amigo*. You turn here. Road closed straight ahead. You turn."

"Okay, *papi*. Next time don't touch a nigga's shit. Wave your got-damn flag 'til you get my attention. Feel me?"

"*Si, Amigo*. I just do my job."

"'A'right. Fucking Mexicans! They come over here and get all our jobs and leave the black man fucked up!" Cash was still talking out loud as he let the window up on his Benz. As the Mexican waved at him to make the left turn, Cash noticed a couple of orange cones in the middle of the street as he drove by slowly, trying not to mess his 22 inch rims up in the pot holes.

Cash was back to reality and paying attention to every detail now, from the Mexican directing traffic to the diner being closed. Plus, there were two more Mexicans sitting on the sidewalk, eating lunch.

Looking up in his rearview mirror, he noticed that the Mexican was sending all the other cars in the other direction. Before he could turn his attention back to what was going on in front of him, he finally saw the two agents pull up at the intersection, and the Mexican that was directing traffic had held the white Yukon up. Laughing to himself while blowing the smoke out of his nostrils, he looked back and stuck his middle finger up at the two agents.

As he picked up speed, Cash heard what sounded like gunshots, but he wasn't sure due to his music being up so loud. As he leaned over to lower the volume on the

C.D. player, he felt the car jerk as if one of the tires had blown. Noticing that the front right side was leaning, he became upset, but knew that there was a gas station right up the block.

Looking back up from the C.D. player, he slammed on the brakes when he saw one of the construction workers standing about twenty feet in front of his car. "Yo, what da fuck are you stupid ass Mexicans doing now? Get da fuck outta my way so I can get my tire fixed, you fucking asshole!"

The Mexican was standing in the middle of the street with one hand holding a "SLOW" sign in front of him. The other hand was behind his back with an Uzi, and he opened fire on Cash, while the other two Mexicans that were sitting there eating lunch also had reached in their tool boxes and pulled out two AK-47's and opened fire from the passenger side of the Benz.

Out of instinct, Cash had ducked down and pressed the accelerator to the floor, not caring what was in his way. He had been ambushed and had no way out of this one for sure.

The windshield had shattered and the bullets coming at him from the front had ceased. The Mexican was reloading, not looking at the car coming at him and picking up speed. The car was smoking from the bullets hitting the engine, and no one could see if Cash was hit or not.

Looking down the street, the two agents saw the first man with the "SLOW" sign take from behind his back what appeared to be a gun, and saw him aim and fire at Cash's Benz. Seeing the other two men jump off the sidewalk and take off running and aiming at the passenger side of the Benz was enough to send their police instincts into effect.

The Mexican standing at the top of the hill guiding

traffic pulled out a handgun and started running towards the shooting, not even noticing that the white Yukon was right behind him.

"Mitch, what da fuck is going on? These Mexicans are about to fuck up our big payday! Go! Go! Get down there! We have to save Cash's ass right now!"

"Well, shoot the one in the street before I run his ass over!"

Before the man knew what had hit him, he was dead before he hit the ground. Agent Thomas didn't hesitate. He leaned out of the window and started shooting. The first shot hit the Mexican in his lower back, and the second in his left shoulder, which spun his entire body around. As his body spun around, Thomas had taken aim for one last shot. Simultaneously, the truck hit the Mexican as the bullet hit him right between the eyes.

Without even looking at each other, the two agents high-fived one another as they raced down the hill to rescue the same man they wanted dead themselves.

Cash knew he only had one chance of getting away, and that was to get past the gunman in front. Taking a chance, he quickly stuck his head up and saw the gunman reloading, and he aimed the car right towards him. Before the man could get another shot off, Cash had run dead into him. With the front tire flat, Cash felt the car as it ran over the dead man's body. Cash could hear the gunman's bones cracking under the car, as he kept his foot on the gas pedal.

Not hearing anymore gunfire aimed at him, had him even more scared. He didn't know the location of the other two gunmen. Looking back over his shoulder, he saw the white Yukon coming, and the gunfire wasn't coming in his direction anymore. The two Mexicans had turned and started shooting at the white Yukon coming at top speed.

With their attention on the white Yukon, Cash drove off, trying to get away.

As he turned the corner, he caught a glimpse of more police running out of the police station and joining a mini shoot-out in broad daylight with two crazy Mexicans strapped with two AK-47's with extended clips. The Mexicans were outnumbered and had nowhere to take cover. They put up the best fight they could in their circumstance before they were taken out by the Anderson Police Department.

Chapter 7

A couple of days had passed, and shit was hot within the city limits.

Kim was lying low and was not trying to be seen. The only place she would go was the shooting gallery with Kane. Other than that, she was at the house.

She knew she had to get it together and do it quickly. Kane was depending on her. She knew people in the streets had cared for Jason, but they had bills to pay, and if she didn't pick up the slack and take care of their customers, they would find somebody else to deal with.

As quiet as it was kept, Kim knew just as much as Jason did. The time had come to put everything he had taught her to the test. She made a promise to herself that what had happened to Cash a few days ago would never happen to her.

As she climbed into her queen sized bed and got comfortable, her eyes weren't even closed ten minutes before her phone had started to ring.

"Good evening. May I speak to a Mrs. Strickland?"

"This is she, may I ask who is calling?"

"Yes. This is Detective Carpenter. I might have some good news for you. Would you like to come downtown to the precinct, or would you like for me to meet you somewhere?"

"It must be really important for you to call me this late. A'ight, give me a few minutes to get myself together and I'll meet you at the Walmart on Highway 28."

To Kim, it was strange for anyone to be called out at this time of night, especially in the life that she chose to live. Jason had taught her to always meet somewhere that there was a crowd of people and a lot of cameras. She wanted to call Kane, but knew she didn't have enough time. This information had to be retrieved immediately. Time was of the essence.

She grabbed her vest and her trusty new friends. Kim had two Glocks. She also kept a .32 inside her panties. Life wasn't playing fair, and she refused to be taken out without taking somebody with her. An eye for an eye had become her new motto.

Before stepping out the front door, she paused, realizing the seriousness of what could happen. She peeked out the curtain to see if anything looked out of the ordinary. Being cautious, she remembered what Kane had told her about being incognito, and she jetted out the back door, grabbed her helmet, hopped on her bike and peeled off through her neighbor's driveway.

Knowing that she would probably be there before Carp, she parked her bike and went into the store. While waiting on his phone call, she tried to play it off as long as she could.

There was a woman walking up and down the same aisles that she was; throwing any and everything into her shopping cart. Kim didn't know if it was her paranoia or if it was just a coincidence. Tonight was not the time for all of this to be happening, so she stopped her and asked, "Excuse me, ma'am. Do you work here, or do you have something you need to say to me?"

"Child, what are you talking about?"

"Well, I don't know if you have noticed, but you have been up and down the same aisles I have. Are you following me? Because I'm not a thief if that's what you're thinking."

The lady shrugged her shoulders, rolled her eyes and went around Kim and continued on about her business.

Just as the lady turned the corner, Kim's phone rang, startling her. "Where are you at, Carp?"

"Walking inside right now."

"Come to the entertainment section." She was already on him, making sure that no one else was with him. Making his way to the back, she kept her distance until she felt that the coast was clear. "Carp, whatever you have, it better be good, having me come out this late. A girl needs her beauty sleep."

"Well, to be honest, Kim, it doesn't matter how much sleep you miss. You will always be beautiful."

She couldn't help from blushing.

"But for real, Kim, what I'm about to tell you may cost me my job and both of our lives. This is some inside shit… some department brass shit."

"What, Carp? Please don't beat around the bush."

"Well, the hit on Jason was a message. But the one on Cash was revenge. See, Kim, Cash is involved in some other side shit that neither Jason nor Kane knew about. He got into major debt, and it turned into a major beef. There was a shootout and one of the men killed was an undercover agent. Kane is connected politically, so he can't be touched, and some of the officers knew this, so they formed a team of off duty cops that were willing to take drug dealers off the streets."

"Carp, how do I know you're not with them and they're outside ready to kill me?"

"Kim, I'm gonna be honest with you. I lost my father to the streets, and when I took that oath to protect and serve, I took the words seriously. My son by my first wife was a hustler. I couldn't change his mind. One of the two boys that I told Kane about that was never found... one was my son. My taking sides with those scum bags that killed my son doesn't sit well with me. I'd rather let Cash and Kane kill them all and turn my head."

"I'm sorry, Carp. But why did you bring this to me instead of Kane?"

"If I would've gone to Kane, my head would probably be on a silver platter before the sun came up. Jason is gone. All Kane has is Cash. But if you present this information, he would look at it in a different way. Inside this envelope are names, pictures and addresses of the two officers that came to your home. They will not stop until Cash is dead. Cash killed two of them the other night, but they can't find their bodies."

"Carp, shit happens."

"Kim, this is some real shit, so be careful."

"Thank you for the information. I'll get it right to Kane, and you be careful yourself. There ain't too many good cops left. Whatever side of the law people choose, I'd rather know that the cops are still the good guys. It's the bad ones who mess it up for the rest of y'all. So, Carp, I hope we never have to meet again under any other fucked up circumstances."

"Me too, Kim. I wish we could've met under better circumstances."

"Carp, are you trying to come on to me?"

"No, ma'am. It just eats me up to see a beautiful young sister have her life destroyed by these streets."

Getting on her bike, Kim noticed two black Yukon's crank up and their lights come on. She wasn't sure if they were going to follow her or Carp.

As Carp got into his Crown Vic, he wasn't paying attention to the two black trucks as he pulled off. They gave him enough space so he couldn't recognize the tail. Even though there wasn't that much traffic at 3:00 in the morning, there was enough for the two trucks to camouflage themselves with Club 28 and Simones letting out at the same time and everyone racing to Hardee's.

Pulling up to a red light, Carp noticed two females beside him waving. Being a flirt, his attention was sidetracked as the two females put on lip gloss, and then leaned over and tongue kissed each other. He was sidetracked to the point where he didn't even notice the men getting out of the first truck and creeping up on him.

When the girl on the passenger side opened her eyes, she froze in a state of shock. Pointing her finger towards the back of Carp's Crown Vic gave him enough time to see one of the men in his passenger side mirror. Reaching for his gun saved his life.

The first shot shattered the driver side window. The female driver hit the gas pedal and pulled off, not looking back. The first shot missed Carp due to him reaching for his gun. The next shot hit him in the back. As the man opened the door and took aim, Carp got two quick shots off into the man's chest.

On the passenger side, the other man started shooting

through the window. Thinking he had hit his target, he emptied his clip and turned to run back to the truck. Upon reaching the truck, he saw one headlight coming straight at him at tremendous speed. Not sure of his next move had cost him his life.

Kim slammed on the brakes and stopped directly in front of him, pulled out her baby Glock and put two in his face.

The driver of the other truck had pulled off with his wheels smoking.

Not sure if Carp was dead or alive, Kim ran up to the driver side and saw another man sprawled out on the yellow line and slightly moving. Realizing it wasn't Carp, she put one in his face.

"Carp, are you okay?"

"Yes. They knocked the wind out of me though. I had my ol' trusty vest on."

"I see blood, Carp!"

"Yeah. I took one in the shoulder, but I'm good. Go... go catch that other truck. Be careful, Kim!"

Racing up the highway doing a buck twenty, she saw the black Yukon. Zipping in and out of traffic, she was close enough to tail it. When the truck made a left onto Main Street, she figured she knew where they were headed.

The bike blowing past the truck at top speed and not slowing down made the driver a little more comfortable. He wasn't sure if it was the same bike from the shooting. The more he kept his eyes on the bike, the smaller the tail lights got until it was finally out of sight.

Slowing down to the speed limit, the two officers knew things had not gone according to plan. While they made their way back to the precinct, they tried to figure out what had happened.

Pulling into the parking lot, the driver got out and lit a cigarette, while the other officer went to take a piss. As the driver took a puff off of his cigarette, he didn't notice the woman walking up behind him. Before he could fully turn around, Kim had put two into his chest. As the other officer tried to put his dick in his pants, she was already coming around the back of the truck. Wasting no time, she shot him once in his dick, since it was still hanging out, and twice in his face.

"Freeze! Drop your weapon and turn around!"

Turning around, she didn't anticipate the security guard in the parking lot making his rounds. She dropped her gun and turned around. With one hand, she grabbed the other gun from her waist and fired three multiple shots into the man's chest. Grabbing her other gun off the ground, she ran and hopped on her bike, and was gone with the wind.

Chapter 8

"Aye yo, Kane! Look at this shit on the news!"
"Turn it up, Country."

"...Good evening. This is Tonya Wilson for Channel Six Eyewitness News. Last night there was a gang-style shooting on Highway 28. A routine traffic stop by four undercover agents resulted in their lives being taken. Another officer pulled up on the scene and was also gunned down, but he will pull through. According to eyewitnesses, the assailants jumped out of a car and ambushed the agents. Then, numerous other gang members rode up on motorcycles and started shooting them from behind, leaving the officers trapped in their trucks and fighting for their lives. The police are investigating this matter to figure out if this was in any way related to this week's earlier shooting in front of the police department, but there are still no leads."

"The ongoing investigation of these latest homicides has caused an uproar in the community. Anderson County has never seen anything of this nature. The gangs are moving in and are fighting over turf."

"Four Hispanic men who appeared to be dressed as construction workers opened fire on two undercover agents and took on the entire police force with no regard for the law. Only one officer was injured in the gangland shootout earlier this week, and last night as I said, four of Andersen City Police Department officers lost their lives for what they believed in."

"More information will be released later. If you have any information regarding this or any other incident, please call 911 or your local police department immediately."

"Back to the studio…"

"Oh shit! Whoever pulled that off, I would love to put them on the team."

"Shut up, Cash. I'm already on the team," Kim responded.

"Fuck you mean?"

"Kane, I need to speak to you right now!" Kim said.

"Excuse us, guys. Step out for a minute."

As everyone exited the room, Kane was watching Cash very closely. "Kim, what's up with you and Cash? Y'all two are at it all the time."

"Kane, listen. Nothing is up with us. But I'm gonna be honest. When you got locked up, I met Cash at the club one night and he tried to holla at me. I'm not gonna front, we went out a couple of times, but he thought he was gonna hit and split. And no, he didn't hit. I know what you're thinking. I'm not one of those 'hood rats that he thought I was. When he realized he wasn't gonna get none, he stopped calling."

"About two months had gone by, and me and my girls had went out to a club in Greenville called Escalades. 50-Cent was performing. I was at the bar and Jason offered to buy me and my girls drinks. I didn't know they knew each other. Me and Jay was together for three months before I gave him my virginity, and we have been together ever since. The night you came home was the first time I saw Cash in six months, and he tried to dis me, and Jason checked him. That night when we got home, I told Jason everything, and he told me not to worry because he loved me."

"I knew it was something with y'all."

"No, it's nothing with us... it's him. He needs to let the past go. But, enough about him. That shit on the news..."

"What about it?"

"Kane... that was me."

"What?"

"Kane, Carp brought me some information on what's going on. The attacks on Jason and Cash were a hit. Here are the envelopes—"

"Wait a minute, Kim. What da fuck happened last night?"

As she explained in detail everything that had happened, the shit Cash was involved in started making sense. Now, Kane began to understand what was going on. Looking up at the video screen, he noticed Cash leaving the office. "Nut, come in here, now!"

"What's up, boss man?"

"Where da fuck is that nigga, Cash goin'?"

"He said he had some unfinished bizness to handle."

"You and Country find that nigga and stay on his ass like glue, you hear me?"

"Gotcha, boss."

"Kim, you feel like clubbing tonight?"

"Whatever, bro."

"Welcome to Bouncers. Would you like a private room or our VIP section?"

"Neither. Take me to the owner's office."

"Sir, Mr. E-Dubb isn't here."

"Bitch, I don't have time for games! Tell him Big Kane is in the building!"

"Yes, Sir."

Within minutes, Kane and Kim where entering the office.

"What's up, Big Kane?"

"What's up, lil' cuz? Did JB send you that info?"

"Yeah, yeah, I got that right here. Man, what the fuck is going on? Those prints belong to some undercover agents. You know I had to work my magic. But enough of that. What's up with this piece right here?"

"Chill! This is my lil' sister!"

"Sister my ass!"

"Nigga, this is Jason's wife, and she's part of the family!"

"She got to be gangsta, 'cause this is the first time I've seen you without Nut or Country. Anyway, let me apologize. I meant no disrespect."

"None taken. My name is Kim."

"A'ight, nice to meet you."

Kane and E-Dubb go way back. Kane met him while doing his bid. JB and Kane used to work for him. He was one of those straight up officers. He didn't give a fuck about anything. As long as you weren't some hot ass nigga, he would fuck with you. Even though he wouldn't bring anything in, he'd let you live in the kitchen.

E-Dubb was one of those officers who was from the streets. His entire family was in the game, but he managed to make it out without getting caught. He owned a strip club under another name, and always showed Kane and JB flicks of the hoes at his club before he hired them.

After checking up on him, he knew Kane was doing his thing in Anderson, and that he was a thorough dude. Kane had sent him some of his baddest bitches when Bike Week came to Myrtle Beach.

Kane wanted to branch out with E-Dubb and open up a strip club called Shakers and Bouncers. He wanted to have the baddest bitches in the South, and then open up another club with nothing but white women. When they both were in prison, they promised to do business together when they got out.

"E-Dubb, I have a proposition for you that might cost you your club, but everything we talked about will come out of the deal."

"Shit, Kane! If more money is to be made, I'm with it!"

"You still work at the prison, right?"

"Yeah. What's up?

"Well, we have a big baller bash coming up, and we need you to invite a bunch of the officers from the precinct."

"Man, what the hell you got up your sleeve?"

"Man, are you in or not?"

"You know I'm in."

"A'ight, I'm gonna hit you up in a couple of weeks, but until then, keep me informed on what's poppin' out there."

As they turned and walked away, E-Dubb couldn't help but stare at Kim. He imagined how her five foot five frame would look in some six inch heels, shaking her ass and sliding up and down on a pole. Even though he was into redbones, her pecan tan complexion and green eyes gave her an exotic look.

Looking over her shoulder, Kim caught E-Dubb staring and put an extra twist in her hips.

E-Dubb started smiling and grabbed his crotch. Running a strip club has its benefits; he could get some head and pussy at the same time. Reaching the back door, he stood in the doorway and called the first chick he saw walking by. "Steph, com'ere!"

"Yes, Daddy?"

"Go get Lexus and the both of you come back and make me happy." E-Dubb knew that they weren't Kim, but right now they would do.

Back outside, Kim and Kane sat in his new black 2009 Range, contemplating the next move.

"Kim, have you heard anything from Carp? You need to find out what else he knows. We need him on our side right now."

"Well, I have his personal cell phone number. As far as him turning or joining us, I don't think that will happen in our lifetime."

"Baby girl, I beg to differ. I think I know who knows where his son's body can be found."

"Kane, you never cease to amaze me!"

"Give me a second." Stepping out of the truck, he began to punch a number into his cell phone, and suddenly noticed something out of the ordinary. What he saw made him jump back into his truck. It wasn't that anyone saw him, because he and Kim had just driven the truck off the lot that day. He always switched up vehicles. "Kim, is that Cash going up in the club?"

"Yeah! Where da fuck is Country and Nut at, Kane?"

Dialing Country's phone, he asked where they were. Country explained that he had just pulled up to the club and was watching Cash go in.

"Well, stay on him, Country. Where is Nut?"

"Nut said he had some other shit he needed to check up on."

"What is he driving?"

"The black Impala. Oh yeah, Cash stopped by the warehouse out by the old airport."

"A'ight, stay on his ass. Something is fishy with them two niggas." Kane knew that shit was getting ready to go haywire. Not sure who he could trust, he made a phone call. "Hello, may I speak with Mr. Rooney?"

"May I ask who's calling?"

"Yes. Please tell him that Mr. Woodson is calling."

"Hey, Kane! This is Mrs. Rooney. How have you been lately? Sweetie, he's not here right now, but is there anything you need me to relay?"

"Yes. Just let him know I called and to return the call as soon as he can."

"Well, it will be a couple of days. He's out of the country. Is there anything I can do? You know it's been a minute, Kane, since I had my itch scratched!"

"I have a few things to handle, but I'll be free in a few hours. Are you gonna to be ready this time?"

"Kane, I stay ready. Plus, I have some information that you might need. Be careful, boo. I'm gonna wear something very special and sexy for you."

Kane knew that sleeping with Mrs. Rooney was one of the biggest accomplishments he could have achieved in his life. When things got rough with Mayor Rooney, Kane would talk to his wife about anything he needed done.

Kane and Mrs. Rooney's first sexual encounter was truly an accident. Mayor Rooney had invited Kane and Country to his inauguration ball. Everybody that was important was there. While everyone was mingling, Mrs. Rooney was getting her drink on. Everyone at the party was drinking champagne, while she was drinking Patron. The more she drank, the hornier she became. Not having sex with her husband was not helping matters in any kind of way. The closer she got to Kane, her heart started beating faster, and she could feel the moistness between her legs. She started fidgeting as she stood there fantasizing about what it would feel like to have this 6 foot 7, light skinned brother making love to her.

Unknowing, Kane just kept on mingling. A few minutes had passed before he noticed that Mrs. Rooney couldn't stop staring at him and licking her lips.

Mayor Rooney had received an emergency phone call that had to be taken in the back. As soon as the mayor left, Mrs. Rooney took advantage of the situation. She approached Kane and asked him to step into the kitchen. "Excuse me, Mr. Woodson. I'm Mrs. Rooney, and my pussy is very wet at the moment. I've been staring at your fine red ass all night, and I would love to feel you inside me right now."

Before he realized what was happening, she had grabbed his hand and had it up under her dress, rubbing his hand back and forth until he slid his massive fingers inside of her. As she stared him in his eyes and grinded on his fingers, she bit her bottom lip as she began to cum on his hand. She began to breathe rapidly and almost started to scream, but Kane covered her mouth and muffled the sound. With her free hand, she started rubbing his manhood, still in his tuxedo pants while sucking two of Kane's fingers. Her moans of ecstasy were elevating to a point where Kane knew that at any second they would get caught.

Mrs. Rooney was so mind blown and didn't care anymore, that she started tugging on his zipper, trying to pull his dick out, so she could put all ten and a half inches in her mouth before letting him get away. As she dropped down to her knees, Kane quickly stopped her. It wasn't that he didn't want her; he was more concerned with someone walking in and seeing this middle-aged white woman on her knees giving a 6 foot 7 black man a blowjob.

"Mrs. Rooney, stop! Please, stop! This isn't right!"

"What do you mean, Kane? I want it right now! I might never get another chance to be with another fine ass black man with all that's going on in my life. Is it that I'm ugly? Am I too old? Please don't do me like this. This is a fantasy of mine."

"Okay, Mrs. Rooney. Get up, please. It has nothing to do with your age. And trust me, you are far from ugly. For your age, baby girl, you look better than the average twenty year old. But I don't think its right. When we do it, I want you to be able to enjoy every inch and every moment."

"Well, could I meet you at a hotel tonight?"

"No problem. Here's my card. Call me later."

As Kane walked away, she slapped him on his ass and smiled, knowing that in a few hours she would have one of the best sexual experiences that a white woman could ever have in her lifetime… a black man.

Chapter 9

A few hours had passed, and Kane's phone had started to ring. "Who dis?"

"E-Dubb. Cash just left here. He didn't even come in the back and holla at me."

"*What?* He left with a bitch or something?"

"Nah, that's the crazy thing about it. The nigga didn't even get a lap dance. He was out there talking to two white dudes."

"Two white dudes? What da fuck is dis nigga into?"

"I got their plate number. They pulled off together, headed in the same direction. The plate number came back registered to the police department."

"Good looking, E-Dubb. I got you in the morning."

"Kim, wake up, baby girl." She had dozed off while waiting on Kane. "This nigga, Cash was at Bouncers talking to two undercover agents, and the nigga left with them following him. I'm getting ready to go meet with Country. I want you to go to the house and wait for my call. As a matter of fact, go ahead and put my number on speed dial, just in case, so that you only have to hit one button, feel me?"

"Kane, you be careful, bro!"

"Country, have you heard anything from Nut?"

"Nah, but you know the Impala has the On Star system in it."

"Damn! When... never mind. What, I just hit this button and they'll tell me where the car is?"

"Yeah, but if you do that, they'll know we're looking for the car."

"You're right. Let me hit E-Dubb up. You know that nigga can find out anything."

As E-Dubb's phone rang, he picked it up with an attitude. "Man, who dis? I'm getting some head right now! You better make this good!"

"Yo, E-Dubb, I need a favor right quick. I need you to tap into On Star and let me know where my black Impala is located. It's a 2008 model under the name of Tyrone Biggs, and the plate number is TTD-1028."

"A'ight, give me a few minutes and I'll hit you right back. Get your ass up, Lexus!"

"Country, something isn't right, man. Cash with two white agents, Nut just disappeared, Jason is dead, the detective had been shot at, and to make matters even worse, these muthafuckers are probably after us too. Then, you got Kim who has killed some muthafucking cops. Man, this shit is bigger than me. If it's about running this town, no one will be able to take me out. If they want me back on the streets, then they got it. You strapped, Country?"

"You know it, big homie! Boy, Kane. It's been a long

time since we've put in any work together. Man, are you still cut out for this?"

"Nigga, are you tripping? Still cut out for this? Wait 'til I find Nut. I'll show you cut out for this!" He was interrupted by his phone. "E-Dubb, what you got for me?"

"It's parked outside of a residence. It's been there for a few hours. The address is 105 Gilmore Road."

It didn't take long for them to find the address. Pulling onto Gilmore Road, Kane noticed that there were only a few houses on the road, and there was enough space in between each one so that no one could hear a thing from their neighbors.

Parking at the end of the driveway, Country and Kane made their way to the double-wide trailer. Once they got close enough to the house, they began peeking in the windows. They were shocked when they saw Nut in the living room with his gun out on the table. Looking around for signs of anybody else, they saw no one.

All of the sudden they heard a loud scream come from the back. Shifting positions, they ran to the back of the trailer where Nut had gone and turned the light on.

"Oh shit, Kane! I thought that nigga had put Kwantie on the plane!" Country exclaimed.

"Country, what the fuck is going on?"

Kwantie's screams interrupted their conversation. "Fuck you, Nut! Let me go! I won't say anything! I'll go back to New York and won't tell Kane anything!"

"Bitch, I don't give a fuck about Kane! When I finish with them niggas, Kane and Cash, they both will be dead or in jail. That nigga, Kane thinks he's untouchable. I could have killed him at any time. And as for that nigga, Country,

I'll put two in his ass if he gets in my way. See, bitch, the only thing that I have your ass for is a free getaway. You're so fucking stupid. You should have fucked with me instead of Cash. He only fucked you because he was trying to get back at Kim. But don't worry. I'll kill you in the quickest way."

"I hate you, you bitch ass nigga!"

While Nut was in the back talking shit, Country had picked the lock on the sliding glass door, and he and Kane had slipped in and were sitting on the couch waiting for Nut to come back into the room.

Arguing with Kwantie had taken Nut off his guard for a few moments. As he was walking back into the living room, he didn't see the two men sitting on the couch. He had walked right past them and went to the entertainment system to turn the radio up. At first when he turned around he thought he was seeing ghosts. "What's up, Country? What's up, Kane? What da fuck y'all doing out here?"

"Nigga, we was gonna ask you the same thing."

Nut looked at the gun that he left on the table and thought about going for it.

"Don't even think about it. You're wasting your time. We already done emptied the chamber and the clip. I want to ask you one damn question. Why would you bite the hand that feeds you?"

"Fuck you, Kane! Nigga, I want to be a boss of my own army, not keep on working for you."

"Let me explain something to you. That's what's wrong with you young muthafuckers today; no respect and no order. In order to be a great boss, you have to be a great worker, and in order to be a great leader, you have to be a great follower. See, some people are born to be bosses, some to be killers, some to be hustlers, some pimps… and then there's your type, the fucking scum of the earth, snitch ass niggas. I don't understand. I make sure you drive the fastest cars on the streets, drive the most expensive shit, wear the finest shit, your jewelry is top of the line, you fuck the baddest bitches, you fly anywhere in the world for free, and your kids are in private school, and this is how you show love? This is how you repay loyalty? Country, do you have a problem with the way you're eating?"

"Hell nah! I have a cool million in the bank just from killing niggas. Man, fuck this dope fiend ass nigga, Kane! This one's on me."

Before Nut could respond, his lights were out. Kane had caught him with a left hook that rocked him straight to sleep. "Country, you got some rope in the truck… better yet, untie Kwantie and tie this piece of shit up in the kitchen. Take that duct tape and tie his right hand over the eye of the stove."

Back in the other room, Kwantie heard all of the commotion and was happy to hear Kane's voice, but she wasn't sure if he was in on it or not until she heard him tell Country to untie her and tie Nut up. She sat there waiting for them to walk through the door. "Kane, thank you, baby! He said he was gonna kill me, then kill you and Country. Baby, where is Cash at?"

"Right now, Kwantie, that's not important. But I promise you I'll get you home safe. Kwantie, don't lie to me. From what you know, what is Cash involved in? There are some heavy hitters looking for him."

"Baby, I'm not sure, but I heard him on the phone one night speaking to someone with a Spanish accent. Then, a dude he met one time had 'MS-13' tattooed on the back of his head."

"Was his name José?"

"Yeah, and Cash owed him an ass full of money. Every time you went out of town he would still have dope of some kind."

"Listen, baby. Sit in here unless you want to watch. Did Nut touch you in any kind of way?"

"No. I think the nigga's gay or something. He didn't try doing anything to me sexually."

"Kwantie, don't lie to me. Did this nigga do anything to you?"

"No, Kane. I wouldn't lie about anything like that."

Making their way back to the kitchen, Country and Kane stood over Nut, staring at him for the first few seconds while debating on what they were about to do to him. Country threw cold water in his face to wake him up, and Kane slapped him so hard he thought he had broken his neck.

While trying to shake it off, Nut spit the blood from his mouth into Kane's face.

Laughing at Nut, Kane wiped his face and licked his hand while smiling. "Nut, is there anything you need to tell me before we go on? Because I have a few questions for you. First off, what do you and Cash have going on? Second, where is Detective Carp's son's body at? Next, were you really going to kill all of us and run the town? Who put your ass up to this? And last but not least, what do you want to be buried in?"

"Fuck you, Kane, you bitch ass nigga!"

"Oh well! Country, turn the stove on low." Looking in the refrigerator, Kane grabbed a Juicy Juice and sat back.

Nut was a true solider, but now he was on the other side. These were tactics that he never knew Kane could conjure up in his mind. The pain from the low flame on the stovetop intensified as Country started turning the knob up. By the time Country had turned the knob to the medium position, Nut had started screaming at the top of his lungs, but the music drowned out his screams of agony and pain.

The smell of burning flesh smelled horrible, but that didn't stop Kane.

Chapter 10

"Who is it?"

"Kim, its Cash. Open the door. Kane sent me out here to pick you up."

Hearing that, she opened the door and didn't even pay Cash any attention. She turned and started walking back down the hallway to go and put some more clothes on.

But it was too late. Cash was immediately turned on. Standing in the doorway watching her walk back down the hallway with her tight boy shorts and cut-off shirt on made his hormones start racing. Kim wasn't even paying him any mind as he stood there undressing her with is eyes. "Kim, what's up? What happened to us?"

"Cash, what do you mean? You thought I was some kind of groupie ass bitch, but I wasn't. I was a virgin, and I was really feeling you at that time."

"Bitch, stop lying!"

"I know you didn't just call me a bitch! I done told you

about your mouth, Cash! If Jason was here you wouldn't be talking to me like that!"

"Fuck that dead ass nigga! It's *my* world now!"

Kim couldn't believe what she had just heard, and before she had a chance to run it through her brain, it was too late. Her mouth dropped open, and before she could duck, Cash hit her with two jabs to the head, knocking her unconscious.

Not caring about anyone else but himself, he picked her up off of the floor, carried her into her bedroom, and stretched her out on the bed. After pulling her boy shorts off and ripping her shirt and bra off as well, he tied her arms and legs to the bedposts and climbed on top of her.

As she started coming to, Cash began pushing himself in and out of her with so much force that it made her gasp for air. Gathering her senses, she tried to fight him off but she couldn't move her arms. She tried to move her legs, but realized that they too were tied to the bedposts. Screaming at the top of her lungs only seemed to make the matter worse. It seemed like her screams were motivating him even more. She tried her best to buck her body to get him off, but his weight and the position that he was in caused him to bury himself deeper inside of her until he felt himself about to cum. His thrusts became more vengeful. He had become more hostile and dangerous.

Her voice had become silent. She couldn't believe that the man who called himself her fiancé's brother was on top of her without a care in the world. Praying for her life, she saw a white light just before she had passed out.

When he finished, Cash got up, kissed her on the lips and walked out saying, "You stupid ass bitch! All you had to do was just give me some pussy and we both would have enjoyed ourselves. Oh well! This will be my town in a few days."

Thinking out loud and talking to himself made him feel like the big dawg. "Damn, Jason! I know why you kept her now. That thing was good and tight, dawg. You know how we do. We share everything. Lil' bro, I kept it in the family. I wish you were here so we could have switched!"

"Kane, please turn the fire off, okay? I'll tell you everything!"

"Turn it down, Country, and let me hear what dis piece of shit has to say."

"Man, promise me that you'll take care of my daughters. You know their mother is a crack fiend."

"You have my word on Jason."

"A'ight, listen man. Cash had got some dope from the Mexicans and thought that he could flip it before you got back. He tried to, but he couldn't get it all done before you came back. When they came to collect, he called me instead of Country. When we went out there to meet them, it didn't go as we planned. They tried to make a deal with us, and Cash shot one of them. You know how hot headed he is. When we made it back here, one of the Narcs on the case confronted him and tried to extort him, so he shot him and took him to JB's."

"Well, what about Detective Carp's son?"

"Big Country, you know the warehouse where we saw Cash at earlier out by the old airport? That's where he took him, but I don't know which bin he's in. Cash put me up to killing you, Kane. He said if I kill you and Country, that I could be in charge and run the town under his name. Kwantie was a bonus. When he told me to take her to the airport, that meant for me to kill her. He said he couldn't trust her. But I kept her alive just in case, for a ticket out of here if shit didn't go right."

"Well, I guess shit didn't go right. But a long time ago I promised you that I wouldn't kill you."

"Thank you, Kane, man. I'll get my daughters and get the fuck outta town."

As they continued talking, Nut was watching Kane's every movement as he pulled out his 50 cal and set it on the kitchen counter, and put on a pair of Latex gloves. "Kane, what are you doing? You said you wasn't gonna kill me!"

"Don't worry, cuz. I'm not. Kwantie, kill this piece of shit!"

The sound of the 50 cal exploding until the clip emptied had Country shocked, because all of the bullets went into Nut's body. She did not miss a shot. Country looked at Kane with a deadly grin. "Better Aiming Shooting Gallery, boss man?"

"You already know, Country. Me and Kwantie have been fucking ever since I came home. Cash had something good at home and he didn't even know it. I took her under my wing. Let's just say it's been over a year since they've had sex."

"Boss man, you's a smart muthafucka! What we gonna do with the body?"

"I would say send him to JB, but we'll give him a nice going home because of his daughters. But that nigga, Cash… that's something different. Kwantie!"

"Yes, Daddy?"

"Are you a'ight? Because I need you to take the Impala and go to Kim's house and wait for my call. We're getting ready to go to war with the biggest and illest gang in the streets."

"Baby, I'm okay. I know you're not talking about going to war with the Mexicans!"

"Nah, the police, baby. I'm not worried about the

Mexicans. They're all about business. All I have to do is pay the debt off and clear our family's name. I just need to find out who killed Jason first."

"Okay. Just promise me that when you catch Cash I can participate."

As they exited the house, they left Nut's body there until everything blew over.

Kane couldn't figure out how to contact Detective Carpenter while he was in the hospital and under heavy security. Then it came to him. He remembered a chick from back in the day that he used to mess with, and who worked in the hospital. Going through all the names on his caller ID, he found her number and called her up. "Hello, may I speak to Angela?"

"This is she."

"What's up, baby? Long time no talk to!"

"What do you want, Kane? I'm at work."

"That's good 'cause I need a favor."

"What's in it for me?"

"Some good dick and five grand."

"Five grand? Who do I have to kill for that kind of money? You know I'll do it for that dick alone, the way you be having me screaming. You gonna give me some while you're up here?"

"Yes, baby. Whatever you want and whenever you want it." Kane was a smooth talker and knew he had Angela's heart. "Angela, give me a few minutes. I have to make one stop and I'll be on my way, baby."

"What's a few minutes, Kane? I know your few minutes!"

"Okay, give me like two hours and I'll be on my way."

"Just call me when you're about to pull up, and be careful, boo!"

Mrs. Rooney picked the phone up on the first ring, not even giving it a chance to ring again. She was not about to miss out on her itch getting scratched. "Hello!"

"What's taking you so long to open the door? Me and Country are standing outside in front—"

Before he could finish his statement, the door opened. Mrs. Rooney was standing there on the steps with red high heel pumps on, a red and white lace negligee and a blue see-through robe on.

The other woman who stood by her at the door had nothing on but a black and pink Victoria's Secret panty and bra set. She immediately grabbed Country's hand and led him to the back of the mansion, as Mrs. Rooney motioned her finger for Kane to follow her up the stairs.

With every step she took, it seemed like she was floating. Her auburn reddish hair gave her a look of elegance which blended with her in-house tan. Mrs. Rooney enjoyed every time that she and Kane could be together ever since their very first time. As they reached the top of the stairs, she turned and put her arms around his shoulders and kissed him ever so passionately.

Lifting her up, she wrapped her legs around his waist while he carried her into the master bedroom. Time was of the essence, and he knew that he had to give her what she wanted and the way she wanted it in order to get the information he needed.

"Kane, you know I'm falling in love with you, right? The way you make me feel inside when I'm around you lets me know that I really want to be with you. The things I'm willing to do to be with you don't even make sense, but no matter what, I know I love you to death. Whether we have sex or not tonight, I just wanted you to have this information."

"Are you okay, baby? I love you too, but you're starting to scare me. What is it?"

"Baby, I want you to make love to me tonight. I want something special between us. Can you do that before you leave?"

She didn't waste any time. Before he could get another word out, she had already dropped to her knees and had him in her mouth. Watching her head bob back and forth and up and down made him grab her auburn reddish hair and move it to the side just so he could get a clear view of her face while she sucked him off.

Noticing the clock on the wall, he knew he was pressed for time and had to make sure that Mrs. Rooney got hers. He also knew that he had to have enough energy left for Angela. He pulled out of her mouth, lifted her up, carried her to the bed and laid her down. He parted her legs and began slowly pushing himself into her already swollen lips.

Kane knew she was a real screamer. The louder she got, the harder and deeper he went into her. He became more excited and turned on the louder she got. He felt her begin shaking like he had never felt her shake before. This was more than her regular nut. Usually he would hit her in the doggie style position, but tonight he was giving her what she asked for. Her legs were on top of his shoulders, and he was deep inside of her, grinding her insides. To him there was nothing special about the way he was fucking her, but to her it was some real tough street thug lovemaking that she had never experienced.

"Kane, that's it, baby! That's it, right there! Oh my God, yes, Kane! Get it, baby! Hit right there! Deeper, baby! I'm about to have an orgasm! Oooo, stop! Don't move, baby! Shhhh! Be quiet, baby. Just hold me tight."

While driving, Country was still thinking about his sexual encounter with the mayor's secretary. At the moment his mind was preoccupied and he was not thinking about Kane.

Kane was too busy looking through the manila envelope and at all of the faces in the pictures that Mrs. Rooney had given him. He was wondering who they were.

The first few were of himself, Country, Jason, Kim, Nut, and Cash. The next set was of four Latin American men whom he didn't recognize. The next set of pictures was of Thomas Howe and Mitch Crimson, whom he didn't recognize. But there was a note attached to their pictures in Mrs. Rooney's handwriting:

Kane, if you are reading this, that means you really must have put it on me real good (smile, baby! Lol!)

These two men's names are Mitch Crimson and Thomas Howe. They are undercover federal agents working with the local authorities to put a case together against you and your crew. My husband is trying to cross you out, and I love you too much to see anything happen to you. These are also the two men who killed your brother, Jason.

As far as Cash, well, he wants to take over the city but he needs you out of the picture to do so.

Be careful, sweetie. I don't trust any of them. But there is an officer that you can trust. His name is Carpenter. Detective Carpenter (Carp) is a real cop. He plays by the rules and he's not crooked. I give you my word on that. If you haven't gotten in contact with him yet, hurry and do so because he's next on the list.

As for the little envelope that's attached to your picture, please do me a favor and don't open it until I tell you to. I want you to put it in your wallet or somewhere safe until I find out the truth.

"Country, man, drive this truck! We have to get to the got-damn hospital as fast as we can. They're trying to kill Detective Carpenter next. We have to get there and save his ass."

"Save the police? Kane, man, what da fuck is going on, big homie? This shit is getting crazier by the second."

"I know, fam. But trust me on this; he's the key to keeping us alive."

"I don't understand what you're saying, Kane. What do you mean by he's the key?"

"Country, it's a long story, but you know I haven't ever steered you wrong and I won't start now. Just hear me out. Carp is a good cop, and the longer we keep him alive, the longer we'll stay out of jail. Listen. I know all of this sounds crazy right now, but fam, we're gonna be okay. Detective Carp is trying to bring down the police force and all of the corruption that's taking place with the crooked ass police officers. The corruption is real big… bigger than what me and you know about. So, if we keep him alive, that will give him room to chase the crooked cops who are working for Mayor Rooney. We'll know when to back down or when to kill his ass. As soon as he starts taking some of them down, then we take him down."

Kane didn't have to say anything twice. Country had gotten the picture and punched his foot to the gas pedal, while Kane got on the phone to call Angela back.

It didn't take long for Country and Kane to get to the hospital. As they pulled up to the back of Anderson Memorial, Country stayed in the truck as Kane made his way to the side door. When Angela opened the service door to the outside, Kane smiled, realizing that he was in the laundry room.

It had been so long since she had seen him that she didn't waste any time. She grabbed his hand and led him to the back room. Before the door could close, she was on her knees, bobbing her head back and forth. Kane's head fell back on the wall as he started enjoying every second of her blowjob.

Angela really had feelings for Kane, but she couldn't deal with his lifestyle. She couldn't stand the fact that he might be here today and gone tomorrow.

Kane felt the same way towards her. He had much love and respect for her, but didn't know how to be with her and only her. The biggest problem he had with her was the fact that she had slept with a bunch of nothing ass niggas, and he didn't want the drama that came with dudes still thinking that she might belong to them.

Every time he looked at her, she reminded him of Nia Long.

Angela continued stroking and sucking his dick even though she knew he was about to cum. Feeling his vein throbbing against her tongue, she just leaned her head back and swallowed every last drop, but she kept stroking, never letting him get soft again.

That was one of the other main reasons that he liked her. She was a freak and knew how to keep him hard the entire time that they were having sex.

Looking at him in his eyes, she licked her lips and kissed the head of his dick before she stood up, turned around and bent over, pulling her scrubs (hospital pants) down and lifting her top.

Kane knew that he was about to love all of this. There was just something about her that he really enjoyed, and it never failed when they were together.

For the first twelve minutes the moans and groans from the thrusting had Angela so wet that Kane couldn't help but to cum again. She felt his body start to jerk, and as soon as he was about to cum she turned and placed him back in her mouth, sucking him clean and tasting her own juices.

Looking at each other, she stood and wiped him off. They kissed, and she handed him a bag. When he went to hand her the money, she pushed it back. Right then he knew the love she had for him was more genuine than any price he could put in her hand.

"Kane, the shit I do for you, I'd get life in prison if they ever caught me. And the crazy part about it, I wouldn't even care just as long as you answer my calls and love me with your heart."

"Yeah, right! You say that shit now. As soon as they get your ass in the courtroom, you would sing like a canary. But you wouldn't ever have to worry about that. I got too much money and too many connections to let anything happen to someone I love."

"Kane, do you really love me, or is it my doggie style and good ass head I be giving you?"

"Girl, stop playing! You know I love you… but that good head helps me love you a whole lot more!"

"Boy, stop playing!"

"Nah, but for real, Angela, I do love you."

Chapter 11

Turning off the highway, Kwantie thought she saw what looked liked Cash's black 750 BMW leaving Kim's neighborhood. Not sure, she sped up, trying to get there and hoping that everything was okay and the car she saw was just a coincidence.

Pulling up in the driveway, she noticed the front door was wide open, and there was no sign of a break in. She nervously pulled out her snub nose .38. Surprise is the worst feeling anyone could have. She didn't call out Kim's name, hoping she would catch the predator in the act. The closer she got to Kim's bedroom, she heard moans of pain. Reaching the doorway, she hoped that the noises were not of her and a man, but what she saw, she'd rather have found her with a man.

"Kimmy! Baby girl, are you okay? Who did this?" While untying the bra and panties that Cash had tied Kim to the bed with, Kwantie recognized the fragrance of the cologne that was still in the air. Saying nothing, she didn't want to push the issue…not right now anyway. Kwantie helped Kim to the bathroom. "Baby, you want to call the police or go to the hospital?"

"No, I'll be a'ight. Kane has enough to deal with right now. Just help me to the shower."

"You want to talk about it?"

"Kwantie, you look a mess yourself. What's going on with you? I thought you were in New York."

"Girl, these Woodson boys keep shit going. I was on my way to New York, and the next thing I know, Nut hit me in the face with the butt of his gun. When I woke up, I was tied to a chair. He had slapped me a few times. He said that Cash wanted to kill me himself."

"For what?"

"I think he found out that me and Kane was fucking."

"*What?* You two?"

"Yeah. Ever since you introduced us at the coming home party, he had kept trying to holla. Cash stopped sexing me, and one day Kane came to the house. I had just gotten out of the shower and walked through the living room in my birthday suit, and was surprised to see this massive man in my living room. Instead of me questioning him why he was standing there, I started walking to my bedroom. He started walking behind me and I didn't stop him. It had been over eight months, and Cash wouldn't touch me, so I did the next best thing."

"Girl, you didn't!"

"No, I didn't do him. I decided to let him watch me. So, I pulled out my toy and started playing with myself. I saw a bulge in his pants, so I grabbed his dick and started stroking it. One thing led to another, and his face was between my legs. It felt so good that I started begging him to put it in and girl…When he did, it felt so incredible. It felt like we were made for each other."

As Kim gathered all her things, Kwantie called Kane to inform him that they were headed to his condo. She also explained that Kim knew about them, so there wouldn't be a reason for him not to come to the condo.

He, in return told her to rent a car and stay in the house with Kim for a few days, because they couldn't risk Cash seeing her and try to finish the job. He didn't want Cash to know that she was still alive. The less Cash knew, the better. What Kane had planned for him was so brutal that it hurt him to his heart to think of killing a family member, especially one as close to him as Cash. Jason was gone, and now Cash had to go too.

"Excuse me, officer. It's time for Mr. Carpenter's vitals to be read."

The officer looked down at the chart to make sure that the names on the two nametags matched those of the people standing in front of him. "Go right in, Doc."

"Thank you, Sir"

Upon entering the room, Carp's eyes opened and almost popped out of his head. Before he could scream, Kane had his hand over his mouth.

"Shhh! Be quiet! I'm not here to kill you. I'm here to let you know that I know where your son is at."

"He's alive?"

"Yes, but I have to get you out of here."

"Why? I'm safe here."

"No, you're not. They're gonna kill your ass. The supposed officer out front doesn't have the correct patch on his sleeve or the right type of shoes on. It's going down. Either you can stay here and die, or I can get you to your son."

"Shit! What are we waiting for?"

"Angela, can we slide through enough rooms to get him out of here?"

"Yes. Take him through the bathroom. Each room has a connecting bathroom. I'll leave and meet you down there."

"Get dressed, Carp."

As they made their way down the hall through the rooms, Angela walked out and continued checking on the other patients as she normally did. The officer didn't ask any questions or get suspicious. When she got four rooms up, Carp and Kane walked out together in regular street clothes.

At first the officer didn't pay any attention, but the size of the second man made him get up and peek into the room. He saw a bulge under the covers, but didn't see the doctor. He pulled out his silencer and screwed it onto his gun and fired at the bulge on the bed. Nothing but feathers flew up in the air. "Damn it!" The man knew that he had messed up and they would have his ass.

After getting off the elevator, Angela led them back the way they had come.

"Angela, thank you, baby! Anything you want!"

"Anything?"

"Yes, anything, baby!"

"Just keep that dick alive. I want to join the Mile High Club!"

He looked at her and smiled. "You got it!"

On the way to the truck, Carp asked, "Kane, what the hell is the Mile High Club?"

"Let's just say it's sex on a plane."

"Boy, you got something going for yourself. She's a keeper. How's Kim doing?"

"Damn! That reminds me, I have to call Kwantie."

When the phone rang, Kim was knocked out so Kwantie picked it up and walked into the living room and explained everything to Kane.

Kane couldn't believe that his own flesh and blood had wigged out over some pussy. But he also knew that pussy and money would be Cash's downfall. Times were really about to get hectic.

Kwantie explained to Kane that Kim wanted him to act like nothing had happened until everything blew over. Kim was gonna stay at Kane's private condo with her. He had bought it a while ago, just for him and Kwantie's private getaways.

Finding Cash wouldn't be simple, so Kane went to the spot for a few hours and texted him with "007", which was their code for an emergency. That meant: Respond, stop what you are doing and come, because something was about to happen. A few hours had passed before he finally responded.

"Cash, where you at?"

"Man, I'm coming up 85 out of ATL. What's up?"

"Man, Nut is dead and Kim was raped. She might not make it. They found her damn near bleeding to death."

"Did she say anything about who did it?"

"Nah, she can't talk."

Chapter 12

"Good morning, sleepy head!"

"The same to you, Kwantie!"

Kwantie had walked in on Kim in the shower. Kwantie was turned on by Kim's sexy body and asked if she needed someone to wash her back. "Yes." Kim mind started to run back to the story of her and Kane having sex and she started getting wet between her legs. Kwantie started washing Kim's back and rubbing lower and lower, Kim let her rub between her legs. Kim held her head back and was enjoying the touch of another woman. Even though she had just been raped a few days ago, Kwantie was touching her in all the right places. Neither had been with another woman, but both had been through hell in the last few days.

Kim reached up and opened Kwantie's shirt and started rubbing her breasts. As their lips touched, they began kissing passionately. Kwantie had undressed and got into the shower with Kim. Turning to face each other,

Kwantie went down on Kim's body with her tongue touching every spot that Jason never knew existed on his woman.

As Kwantie reached Kim's secret box, Kim took her two fingers and opened it for her to lick. With the water running down her body, the tension had built up and she started cumming in Kwantie's mouth. Not stopping, Kwantie had slipped one finger inside herself, trying to enjoy the same pleasure.

Kim got out and grabbed her hand and led her to the bedroom. Laying Kwantie down, she crawled between her legs and licked her all over, returning the favor, until Kwantie had felt her lips being parted and the warmth of Kim's tongue penetrate her moistness. Kwantie started rubbing her own breasts with one hand and fingering herself with the other. Kim liked this reaction so much that she slid her tongue down to Kwantie's asshole and pushed it inside.

Kwantie and Kim fucked and moaned all night. They took turns pleasing each other until they finally cuddled up and went to sleep in each other's arms.

"Kim, what happened last night… I can't explain, but I felt so good!"

"Kwantie, shhh! Just let it be. What happened, happened. And yes, it felt good to me too. But what do we do now?"

"Well, we can keep it as our little secret if you want."

"Kwantie, have you ever…"

"What, Kim?"

"You know. Have you ever been with a woman before?"

"No, but if it feels like that every time, then I might start enjoying myself that way more often. What about you, Kim?"

"No, but it felt so good that I would love to be with you and only you, since Jason is gone."

"For real? Well, I won't disagree, but what am I supposed to do about Kane?"

"I guess you can have your cake and ice cream for now. Just as long as you promise me that you won't ever mess with another woman."

"I promise, Kim, and that goes for you too."

"You don't have to worry about me. I've only willingly been with you and Jason, and since he raped me, unwillingly with that bitch ass nigga, Cash!"

Kissing one another had sealed their relationship.

Nut was a childhood friend that Country and Kane had met on the playground in middle school. A bully had come outside for recess and was taking everybody's lunch money. When he came up on Nut, Nut wouldn't give in, and the bully began pushing him around. Nut had enough heart to stand up to him though. The bully stole a punch that landed on the side of Nut's head. Everyone thought Nut was dazed, but he shot a flurry of punches so fast that the bully turned around and ran away.

Once the fight was over, Country and Kane had introduced themselves as "the schoolyard hustlers". Kane had everything—from candy to school supplies. And because of Nut's height, Kane knew he would be a major factor. With Country and Nut collecting the money and Kane's brains, they had become the most intimidating trio that the streets had ever seen.

After their summer vacation, they moved on to high school. Things were a little different, but the streets already knew who they were. Their reputations had preceded them.

One day after school, Country and Nut had stayed for basketball practice, and Kane decided to hang around. After practice, a fight broke out and Country had stabbed a white kid. When the police arrived, everyone had started running, and Kane had gotten snatched up.

Once in the squad car, Officer Rooney had offered Kane a deal. It involved petit larceny and Kane selling more than candy. Officer Rooney handed Kane a card with his number and a book bag with a pound of weed and one hundred bottles of crack worth twenty dollars apiece.

Kane didn't want anything to do with this so called deal, but he knew that he had no choice, because he would just end up being another missing black child. So, in order to keep his life, he agreed, and Officer Rooney gave him the time and date to call him.

Once out of the car, Kane ran as fast as he could. Officer Rooney had let him out on the north side of Mill Hill. Anyone who wasn't white knew not to get caught in that area once the sun went down.

Once Kane crossed the railroad tracks, he slowed down and caught his breath. Walking down the street toward Country's house, he saw him and Nut sitting on the porch. They couldn't believe their eyes at first, until they saw what was in the book bag. Nut knew how to get rid of the weed, but knew nothing about the crack. But Country had an uncle who smoked and lived around the corner. Once they let Country's uncle hit one of the bottles, he brought them all kinds of business. Nut was selling all the weed, and Country sat at his uncle's crib and sold all the bottles.

Within three days everything was gone, and they had made more than they had planned.

Officer Rooney thought it might take a little longer, so he had given Kane two weeks. But the fiends couldn't wait that long. The trio had built up a clientele and couldn't risk losing it. Kane took a chance and called the number and spoke with Rooney, and it didn't take long before business really started booming.

By the end of the first month they were up to five pounds and a half a kilo of cocaine. Country's uncle had shown them how to cook it up and turn it into crack. They never had to spend money to re-up. Whatever they needed and whenever they needed it, Officer Rooney would deliver. The trio had blown up. Kane knew with the police on his side that he couldn't be stopped.

As usual, everything was going too good. When you start getting money, the jack boys will come. The only thing about it, it wasn't an outsider it; was Country's uncle.

Kane had bought a new Saab with BBS's, and Country had a black Jetta, while Nut went to the extreme and bought a black Porsche 911. Everybody knew what was going on, but dared not say anything.

Christmas, 1989 had come, and the boys had been in the game for over a year. They were stunting real hard for their ages. Plus, they had the drop on every raid before it happened, thanks to Officer Rooney.

While heading to a Christmas bash, Kane had dropped off the work for Country's uncle and left. The next morning when it was time to get the work, it was gone, and so was Country's uncle. Not knowing what to do, Kane called Rooney and explained everything. Rooney told him not to worry about it, and to meet him at the spot and bring his two homies. The trio was scared to death, because they had never been with Kane before when he met with Rooney.

Time had passed quickly, and the time had finally come. Pulling up to the spot in the country made them even more nervous. When they got out of the car, they all took a deep breath. As they knocked on the door, they heard what sounded like screams of pain and agony.

"Come in, guys!" Rooney shouted from the back.

As they entered, Kane noticed the black Nike gym bag on the table. Trying to focus on what was going on, he was sidetracked when two naked women walked in and led them to the back. Upon leaving the room, the first woman winked and cracked a smile in his direction. Distracted for a few moments, the three didn't even realize how far they had traveled through the house.

"What's up, guys? Are y'all thirsty? Do y'all want anything?"

"Nah, we're good. We just want to know why you called us out here."

"Kane, since you're the spokesman for the trio, I'm gonna start by saying this: Welcome to *mi casa!* But on the real, my shit came up missing, and somebody has to pay."

"Rooney, ain't no need for this, man. We have enough money to pay you."

"See, my son, it's not green I want… its red!"

"What do you mean?"

"Well, somebody has to pay with their life. I just want to know who is gonna sacrifice theirs. See, y'all are playing a grown man's game, and the stakes are a lot higher now."

"Rooney, man, you don't have to kill nobody… not one of us anyway. If you give us a couple of days, I'll find the bastard."

"When you find the bastard, what will you do to him?"

"Man, I'll put two to his dome."

"What about you two knuckleheads? Will y'all put a

bullet in the person who stole from you?"

"Yes."

"Well, all three of you have given me your word. Gentlemen, in this business your word goes a long way. That's all you have is your word, and your balls and your dignity. Follow me."

They made their way downstairs to the basement where Rooney opened the door and turned the light on. They saw a man tied up in a chair. From a distance they couldn't recognize the face because of the beating it had taken. The man's eyes were completely swollen shut. But once they got closer, they knew exactly who it was.

Rooney, without saying anything, nodded to the table next to the man. There were three nine millimeters, one for each of them. "Remember, men. Y'all gave me your word of what y'all would do if you caught this nigga. So, I'm gonna make this as easy as possible. Two of the guns have blanks, so only one of you will actually be killing this piece of shit."

With nothing else being said, they all knew that it was kill this piece of shit, or have Rooney kill them. Without a second thought, they all lined up and took aim and fired until the clips were empty. This had sealed the deal of brotherhood.

"Now, y'all take the black bag upstairs on the table and get that money. For my troubles, add six grand more to the bill. Plus, inside the bag are three more nines. Next time y'all better handle your business!"

"Rooney, don't worry. There won't be a next time. Me and Nut will lay the murder game down. You just keep that work coming to Kane," Country assured him.

"Well, Country, that's the type of shit I like to hear. I also have some news for you. I'm about to run for mayor. Y'all know what that means if I win, right?"

Chapter 13

"Kane, what's going on, man? Who killed Nut?"

"I don't know. They haven't found his body, but the police found the car. What's this shit about you fucking with the Mexicans?"

"Man, that was a side deal I had going on."

"Fuck you mean a side deal? We been in this shit since '88, nigga; me, Nut and Country, and we never dealt with anyone other than Rooney. Nigga, you forget who brought you into this?"

"Nah, but I was trying to make moves outta town."

"Outta town? We can't control shit outta town. Greed can bring any empire down at any time. Man, I lost my brother, my friend, and I'm losing my mind! Carp is on our ass, Rooney is beginning to get scared, and Kim is on her death bed! Man, I need to know where you stand!"

"What do you mean? Cuz, I'm with you 'til the end. Have you heard anything on Kim's attacker?"

"Nah. I sent her to a private doctor. Cash, what's up

with your man? Do you have any info on Carp's son?"

"Carp, this Kane. As soon as you receive this message, call me back." A few hours had gone by and no response from Carp. Kane started worrying. "Man, I'm headed to the condo. You're welcome to come," he said to Country.

"Nah, big homie. Shit is real in da field. I'd rather stay in the streets and keep my eye on Cash. That nigga has a bag full of tricks."

"Well, be careful dawg. Right now, ain't no telling what that nigga might be capable of doing. He's like a wild animal with his back against the wall. If it comes down to you or him, handle your bizness, my nigga. Don't hesitate."

"I feel you, but you know how I handle mine."

Getting off the elevator, Kane always put his ear to the door before putting his key into the lock. Once he felt that the coast was clear he would enter. But tonight was different. The stress and heat had made him break his routine. Putting the key in and opening the door, he saw what he had never thought about.

Kim was lying on the couch asleep, with no panties on and a T-shirt that barely covered her thighs. Not helping but to stare, the man in him made him take a sneak peek, but the gentleman in him made him walk over and pull the covers over her, which woke her up.

"Hey, Kane! What's up? Have you found out anything yet?"

"Yeah, baby girl. Cash finally came back, but I have

my eye on him as of now. Is Kwantie here?"

"Nah. She ran out to get us something to eat. She said she didn't feel like cooking this late."

"You a'ight, Kim? You know I'm sorry for sending you home. But hurry up and get better. We got some work to put in. You know I found Carp's son?"

"Carp's Son?"

"Yeah. He's not dead. That nigga, Cash has him hidden. Oh yeah, do me a favor. When Kwantie comes in, tell her I'm in the shower. As for you, anything you need, make yourself at home. You never have to leave. What's mine is yours," Kane told her, not knowing that those words were going to come back and bite him in the ass.

Kim just smiled and thanked him.

While in the shower, he turned the massager on and enjoyed the only moment in the day that he had to himself.

While Kane was in the shower enjoying himself, Kwantie entered the condo. Even though Kim was practically asleep, she was awake enough to feel Kwantie pull the covers off of her and rub her hands between her legs. Speaking softly, Kim said, "Kwantie, you know Kane is in the shower, right?"

"Don't worry. He'll be in there for damn near thirty minutes."

"Are you sure?"

"Kimmy, don't be scared. Let me kiss it, baby."

Before Kim could deny her request, Kwantie had already parted her legs and was licking Kim's secret box. Kim lifted her shirt and began squeezing her own breasts until her nipples were rock hard. Moaning and licking her own lips, she slid her finger into her juice box and started rubbing her clit.

As Kwantie tongue-fuck Kimmy, she could feel her body tense up and start to climax. As her body began to buck, Kim stared Kwantie in the eyes as she sucked all her juices clean.

Standing up and ready to walk away, Kim grabbed Kwantie by her arm and turned her around. Kwantie was caught by surprise when Kim pushed her down the hall. When they walked by the master bedroom, Kim stuck her hand under Kwantie's tennis skirt and began to finger fuck her, while their tongues touched and held each other. Kwantie stuck her hand under Kim's T-shirt and squeezed her ass cheeks while lifting her leg a little. The shower had completely drowned out the sounds of ecstasy.

"Fuck me, Kim! Finger me, baby! I like it like this! Don't stop, baby!"

Kim, feeling Kwantie start to shake, dropped down and started eating her out, while Kwantie held her lips apart and rubbed her little man in the boat. Cumming all over Kim's face made both of them feel good about themselves. But, the night wasn't over.

As Kim got up and started walking back down the hall, Kwantie slapped her on the ass and smiled. While fixing her tennis skirt, she walked into the bedroom and stripped down to her birthday suit and got in the shower with Kane.

Sitting on the bench and letting the water run down his body had Kane very relaxed. He wasn't expecting Kwantie to come in and want to sex him. Without moving, he watched her get right down on her knees and put him in her mouth. She was really beautiful with her jet black hair, but her trademark was her slanted eyes.

Bobbing her head up and down, and slobbering and stroking at the same time had Kane thinking about Angela. With Kwantie, he was willing to try anything. Looking into her eyes, she stared right back as she did tricks with her tongue around the tip of his head.

The more she stroked, the more she felt the vein in his manhood start to throb. She knew that within seconds he would explode. Doing what she knew he loved, she deep throated him while he released the pressures of the day down her esophagus.

Still stroking and sucking, she made him keep his erection. Realizing that he was still hard, she stood up and straddled him. Wrapping her arms around his neck, she rode him. In her mind she was thinking of Kim, but nothing felt as good as ten inches of a real man who knew how to hit all the right spots.

Moving up and down faster and faster, Kane held her waist while slamming her down hard. He could feel the warmth of her juices run down his thighs, but didn't stop. As she came down, he lifted his hips to meet her.

She couldn't hold it in anymore, and started cumming. She began to shiver and yell.

Kim was in the living room smiling, with the TV turned down.

"Kane, fuck this pussy, baby! Do it! I'm cumming! Don't stop!"

The harder he pushed, the louder she got. Once she collapsed on his chest, he lifted her up and carried her into the bedroom. Soaking wet meant nothing to his chinchilla carpet or his silk sheets. Satisfying her was the most important thing on his mind. A nut was nothing to him. He could get that anywhere.

Making it to the bed, he laid Kwantie on her back and lifted her legs to his chest. Pumping with the same rhythm, they were in the groove. She was rubbing her breasts while he pumped away and sucked on her toes.

Staring at him, she reached down and opened her pussy some more so she could get the whole ten inches inside of her. The moistness had caused his nuts to slap against her butt cheeks.

Looking down, he saw his dick go from chocolate to creamy. Every time she came, she would bite her lips and squeeze her muscles. Before she could finish, Kane pulled out and turned her over on her stomach and went back in her with powerful, deep, thrusts.

Loving every second of it on all fours, she put one hand on the headboard and pushed back. With the other hand she reached under and grabbed Kane's balls. Moaning louder and louder, Kane started pumping faster. Kwantie, who was so turned on by Kim and then having a man like this, told Kane, "Baby, slow down. Do it slow. I want you to put your finger in my ass."

"You sure?"

"Yes, Kane. When you get ready to cum, put it in my ass. I want to feel you inside of me."

As he slow grinded in her and slid his finger in her ass, she lay down and kept her ass up in the air. Looking between his legs, Kwantie saw Kim standing there with nothing on, fingering herself. Kim watching them caused her to tell Kane to put his dick in her ass. He put it in slowly at first, but his cum became a lubricant as she tried to perform for her girl. It took quite some time, but she wasn't going to stop until she could take it with ease.

Deep down inside, she had become what Kane had wanted; a woman in the streets and a freak in the bedroom. Reaching back and snatching him out, she turned and sucked him good one more time.

With her head bobbing, Kane noticed a figure in the doorway through the mirror behind the bed. She had one hand on her breast and the other between her legs. Pulling out of Kwantie's mouth, he pushed her back down. Looking in the mirror while pumping in and out of Kwantie, she wrapped her legs around his waist and palmed his ass until she came. Still pumping, she knew that he was getting ready to bust a blood vessel.

Kwantie watched Kim watching her… at least that's what she thought. Kim had locked eyes with Kane through the mirror. They were both on the same rhythm. Every time he pushed into Kwantie, she would push her finger inside herself.

Kane asked Kwantie if she was ready, only she didn't hear him. But Kim shook her head yes. Releasing everything he had into Kwantie, Kim released at the same time.

Was this a coincidence? Kim asked herself. *Or were we really staring at each other and were on the same rhythm?* She wasn't sure, but watching them every night would make her want some of that ten inches herself. She knew she was wrong for thinking like that, but she couldn't allow herself to be alone with him in the house.

Running back to the living room, she lay down and went to sleep, just as Kane and Kwantie did.

Chapter 14

As the sun rose, Carp had parked his Crown Vic and drove his personal car.

Detective Carpenter was a straight up guy. He grew up in the streets of Harlem. Basketball and hustling were his first loves.

His father was robbed and brutally killed due to the dope game. Everything was a joke to him until that night. He now valued his life a little differently. Carp hated thinking about that night, but after just getting out of the hospital, he began to second guess his career choice and what was going on in it at this point. He lost his father to the game, and now his own life was almost taken due to the game. He couldn't figure out what had taken place or what went wrong. He thought he was different; he was on the other side of the law. What really had him confused was the fact that the streets were protecting him.

While sitting in his black Lexus 400, Carp couldn't get the night his father was killed off of his mind. His father was a true New Yorker. He was born and raised in Harlem, on 121st and Lenox Avenue. During the late seventies and early eighties, heroin ran the streets of New York City. Carp's father was a major player in the game. Working for Mickey Banks had its ups and downs.

There was a rival gang formed by Freddy Lovetts who was putting it down just as big, if not bigger, and his product was equal if not a little better.

Then, Carp's father started getting high on his own supply. One thing led to another, and his money started coming up short. He started cutting the packages a little too much. He also loved the limelight just as his boss, Mickey Banks did. Thus, his flashy and flamboyant lifestyle had caught up with him on a cold winter night on Christmas Eve, 1983. That was the last time Carp would see his father alive. "Mr. Flashy" had a "blind date" with the Reaper and didn't even know it. Carp was just seventeen and still remembered everything as if it was yesterday.

He and his father were on their way back home from the store. As they turned the corner on 121st and Lenox, Carp's father noticed a black Lincoln Continental sitting in front of his brownstone. Seeing the two men sitting in the car with the motor running had caught his attention. Reaching for his gun, he became upset because he realized that he had left it in the house. When he was with his son, no guns or drugs was a promise that he had made to himself. But this was one of those times that he wished he had broken that promise.

Once they reached the front of the house, the two men stepped out of the car and called him over. Feeling nervous, Carp's father knew that one of the men was named Reverend, and everyone knew that if Reverend came to see you, it was not a blessing. He knew that he was a stone cold killer; a hit man for hire or the cleanup man.

"Son, go and take the bag to your mother. I'll be right in."

Not knowing those words would be the last thing Carp would ever hear his father say to him, before walking up the stairs of the brownstone and going into the house. He looked back, trying to catch a glimpse of the two men.

When young Carp closed the door, he turned to peek through the curtains and saw what seemed like fireworks going off in front of their house. Once his eyes were able to refocus, he had dropped the brown A&P grocery bag and couldn't believe what he had just seen. His father was gunned down right in front of their home, and he never got to see the men's faces clearly due to the way his father had raised him to never look at grownups if they weren't talking to you directly.

It took some time, but he finally pulled it together and tried to straighten up his life. That was the day he swore he wouldn't be another statistic of the ghetto. He went back to school and got straight A's and received a scholarship to the University of South Carolina. Once he graduated, he joined the Navy. After four years he went back to South Carolina and promised his mother that he wouldn't do wrong, and gave back to the community. Once moving her down south, she began to enjoy life a little more.

One day while reading the newspaper he saw an ad and applied to the Police Academy. Passing with the highest grades, he immediately joined the force.

A few years had passed, and the streets were slowly but surely cleansing themselves. He played fair in the streets. He always gave everyone a chance if he could. But you couldn't bribe him. He was strictly business and by the book. Once he started getting promotions, he decided to start a family.

Carp knew the Anderson City Police Department was as crooked as they come. He had been made offers, but turned them all down. None of the other officers knew how to take him, so they kept their distance. No one wanted to partner with him. Even the rookies wanted nothing to do with him. It really didn't matter to him, because his work spoke for itself. Also, he could never launch an all-around investigation on the department by himself.

Once his son had become a junior in high school, he was already in the streets. Carp did everything he could to deter him from that lifestyle, but he also knew that you had to let a child go in the world and learn for themselves. But this was a price that had no exchanges with it. Once you're in with the wrong people, there is no getting out.

Carp knew of the Woodson boys, but could never get anyone to speak out about them. His paper trail only showed that Kane had gone to jail for a quarter pound of weed and a Tec-9 He was only sentenced to one year and a day. Six months of that was served in county and the other ninety one days were served at Cross Anchor State Prison.

Cash and Jason were not making enough noise to raise the radar. Country and Nut were untouchable as long as they worked for Kane, who worked for Lt. Rooney at that time.

But now Lt. Rooney was Mayor Rooney, and his paper trail was as clean as they come. Carp didn't have anything on him, and Kane would never speak.

Over the years, the department had gotten sloppy. Two undercover agents had pulled a black Lincoln Navigator over in front of the mall. Carp was sitting in the parking lot waiting for his wife, when he witnessed with his own eyes, one of the officers put a duffel bag in the truck and pulled off. Mitch and Thomas were following the orders of Mayor Rooney. Pickups and drop-offs would happen at any time and anywhere. No questions were asked.

The way it was done; Cash would have one of his soldiers drive whatever vehicle he chose for the day, then he'd call Rooney with the information for the drop offs. Rooney would then in turn call Mitch and Thomas with the information. They knew where to find the car, what time to pull it over, exactly where the bags would be, then they would make the exchange and go on about their business like it was a routine traffic stop and let them go. Depending on how much was to be exchanged, they would meet with Cash personally. But for the most part, it was done this way.

One day while listening to his radio, he heard a call made by the dispatcher. Jotting the plate number down on the truck was the beginning.

A few days had passed before he pulled up right behind the truck. Throwing his blue lights on, the truck had pulled over. When he got to the truck, his heart almost fell out into the street when he saw his son sitting in the passenger seat of Cash's truck. He almost lost his cool.

Walking around to the passenger side and opening the door, he snatched his son out and threatened Cash in front of a lot of young onlookers. "Shawn, what the fuck are you doing in this fucking truck? Boy, I bust my ass every day to keep you away from this mess, and this is how you repay me? You ride around with the same scum that I try to take off the streets? This is the same scum that killed your grandfather! What is wrong with you, Shawn? Get your ass out of this got-damn truck before I do something I might regret to one of these low life niggas out here tonight!"

"Pops, why you trippin'? We're just chillin', man! It ain't like we doing anything. I'm just chillin' with him.

He's one of the sponsors for the basketball team. Man, you out here pulling people over just 'cause you can. You make me sick! Yo Cash, I'ma holla at you later, dawg. You know how my pops be. He thinks everybody is up to no good."

"A'ight Shawn. Hit me up later. Oh yeah, make sure you keep working on that jumper. You might be the next Kobe Bryant! As for you, Detective Carpenter, have a good night, officer!"

"To hell with you, Cash! We will meet again, and next time it won't be so sweet. As a matter of fact, how's your brother? I'll be catching you later. "

Cash just smiled.

Pulling off, Carp vowed that he was going to put one – if not all of the Woodson boys behind bars. Their run in the dope game was too long. Even though they were well connected, he knew that if he could get one of the brothers to talk, the whole empire would crumble.

"Kane, what's going on? Man, I've been tailing Cash for the last hour, and he just pulled up at Bouncers. I'm 'bout to go in. I'll keep you informed."

"Carp, I'll be there in a few. Stay put."

"I'm good, but what about Cash?"

"Don't worry; I can handle him from here." Kane then called E-Dubb and told him to make Cash look very important until he got there. "E-Dubb, are Lexus and Steph there?"

"Yeah. What's popping though? You want me to sic them on him now or wait for you?"

"Nah. Tell them to suck that nigga's ass dry... do whatever he wants except leave. Tell them it's on me."

Jumping out of bed, he kissed Kwantie on the cheek

and got dressed. While walking out of the room, he was on the phone with Country, telling him to meet him downtown at Bouncers.

Stopping in the kitchen to grab a juice, Kim heard him and turned over and pulled her shirt up, exposing her cheeks and her swollen lips. Just as she thought, he stopped right at the foot of the couch and stared for a few seconds, and then grabbed his crotch while licking his lips. She had pretended to waken to see what he would do.

"Good morning, Kane."

"The same to you, baby girl. I'm 'bout to bounce. If you need anything, hit me up, you hear me? *Anything!*" All this was said while he was still looking at her pretty pink lips and hard ass nipples.

As soon as the door had shut, Kim was headed to the bedroom.

Chapter 15

"Welcome to Bouncers. VIP or private?"

"Neither, shorty. I'm here to meet with E-Dubb."

"Who shall I say is here?"

"Tell him it's his cousin, Cash."

Making her way through the curtains, Cash couldn't help but to stare at the hostess' ass. Her thong had disappeared between her cheeks after her first few steps. He thought to himself that he had to tap that before leaving here this morning.

"What's up, cuz? What brings you out this way this early? I thought you were a vampire, nigga, 'cause I only see you at night! Let me check and see if your skin is burning in this sunlight!"

"Nigga, stop fucking playing! Yo, I came by to relieve some stress. Man, I fucked up. I'm supposed to be meeting two guys here today, but I needed to come and make sure the coast was clear. Yo, E-Dubb, have you seen that nigga, Nut? Kane's looking for him. I thought he might of have stopped by. You know how he be tricking. But for starters, send me that thick ass chick who went and got you."

"Who, Lexus? She comes as a package deal. But before I go, the two guys that you're waiting for, what do they look like?"

"Trust me, when they hit the door, you'll know." Walking upstairs, Cash was ready to be sexed by the two women while he waited for the two men.

Outside, Carp had parked in the rear of the club to wait for Kane. He saw the black Range pull up, containing a single person.

Country parked directly in front of Carp and didn't notice the driver in the black Lexus.

All of a sudden, a Yellow Cab pulled up, and Kane paid the driver and got out.

Flashing his headlights to catch Kane's attention, Carp almost caught more than that. Kane reached under his shirt and pulled out a 50 cal. Just in the nick of time, he realized that it was Carp in the Lexus.

Once all three men were in the truck, Carp handed Kane a manila envelope with pictures of two Spanish men in them. A few seconds later, a champagne colored F-150 pulled up. The two occupants of the truck were the same two faces he was staring at in the pictures. Things were starting to fall into place.

Kane turned and explained to Carp about his son.

Carp wasn't prepared for the news he was about to receive. Sitting back, the information had fallen on him like a ton of bricks.

"Carp, I'm not gonna beat around the bush. I

mean no disrespect as I explained. Do forgive me, but that night you pulled Cash over in the black truck that your son was also in, that started the chain of events. Cash told me that he had never felt so disrespected, and promised on his life that he would get revenge. I didn't know it was to the extent of kidnapping your son and torturing him."

"Is that your word, Kane? You didn't know or have anything to do with it?"

"One thing about me, Carp, I stand on my word. Don't ever forget that."

"I believe you. Go ahead, Kane."

"Well, at the time of the kidnapping, I didn't know it was your son 'til I saw it on the news. But I still didn't know that Cash had kidnapped him. Cash is into so much shit that I just didn't piece it together."

"Did he tell you any details?"

"This is how it happened: Cash told your son to meet him at one of our afterhour's spots where all the jitterbugs hang. From what he told me, your son wanted to be in the streets with the dope boys so bad that there wasn't anything he wouldn't do to prove that he was down. Even though you may not know it, your son ain't no wimp. He's not some angel who deserves all the damn praises. From what Cash told me, he has put in work, and he was rising in the ranks of our family at an alarming rate. He's well respected in these streets. He can hold his own out there."

As Kane continued explaining, Carp couldn't believe his ears. Cash had tricked his son to get back at him. Everything he was trying to explain to his son had come true. But stupidity overrides ignorance every time. The more he heard, the more he believed that Kane knew nothing about what Cash had done. Even though he knew only some of the details, Carp was a good judge of character.

"Before I take you to your son, I need to know where you stand. Just listen. Whatever happened between your son and Cash, I didn't order that. He has been operating on his own lately, making my family's name look bad. You see, these two guys in the pictures used to run with our family. Then all of the sudden, they branched out and made their own moves. One thing about this family, you will follow orders, or the orders will be given on you. Understand, I'm not asking you to turn the other cheek, but by sitting here in my truck, you have decided to put your badge on the table and become a vigilante."

"I thought I would never turn the other way, but I'm with you. Just make sure my son is safe."

"Well, one thing for sure is that he will be safe. And I have something for you when this is all over and I'm finally out of the game."

"You have a deal, son. Your father would be proud of you."

"Hold up! You knew my father, Carp?"

"Well, let me say this. That wasn't any accident that they were in. When this is all over, I have some info for you. But right now, let's stay focused."

"Country, call E-Dubb and tell him to show the two gentlemen who just walked in to the 'special room' in the back."

While Country made the call, Kane and Carp made their way to the back of the club. After they were buzzed in, they waited in the office until E-Dubb came back. Country was outside and had hotwired the F-150, and was awaiting further instructions.

In the club, the beautiful black women who walked around naked amazed the two Mexicans. Whispering to the men, one red bone held their attention for a long time by making her ass clap. She asked if they wanted to go to a private room.

Nodding his head, the bigger of the two couldn't resist when she rubbed the bulge in his pants. Making him feel larger than he was, she worked her magic. Licking him on the earlobe and sitting in the other's lap while grinding, they couldn't resist going into the private room.

As they got up and went into the hallway, they passed a couple of rooms before they finally made it to their final destination. When the door opened, the woman dropped her bra and panties straight to the ground and lay on the floor while they took a seat in the two chairs in the middle of the room. While she performed sexual acts on herself, the smaller of the two men pulled out his penis and started stroking himself.

So deep in concentration, neither man noticed the mirror on the wall slide open. Kane and Carp had stepped through the hidden door. As the woman saw them step into the room, she started moaning louder while pushing a bottle in and out of her.

The two Mexicans never saw a black woman in this manner, and were stunned. Knowing this by watching their expressions, she knew that she had their undivided attention, and before they could react to the two towering shadows, their lights were out. Carp had pistol-whipped the men into unconsciousness.

Before leaving out of the secret door, Kane went through their pockets and threw the red bone a couple of stacks. She smiled and winked as she got dressed. "Kane, hopefully I can perform for you. My real name is Giovanni," she said enticingly.

"I'll keep that in mind. Do you go both ways?"

"No, but for you I'll try anything once."

"Well, I know where to find you. But right now, I have some other business."

Once in the Range, they headed to the old airport out in the country. They knew that the woman who looked after the place had no problem giving Kane the key to Cash's storage.

When they pulled up in front of number 299, Carp didn't have a clue as to what was about to happen, but for his son's life, it didn't really matter. He told himself that he would repent and ask for forgiveness. But right now, God had to understand.

When Country lifted the gate, Carp couldn't believe his eyes. His son was tied to a chair in the middle of the room with no clothes on. His face had been badly beaten, but other than that he was in good condition. Cash had to be taking care of him. Carp ran over and untied him.

Before the tape over his mouth had hit the ground, Shawn was apologizing for his stupidity. Putting his clothes on, he hurried out of the room to get some fresh air because the room smelled of feces. Once the fresh air hit his lungs, he began vomiting.

"Country, get them two bastards out of the truck!" Kane ordered.

Carp watched as Country put them in the same predicament they had just seen his son in. Not interjecting, he stood and watched while his son got himself together.

"Kane, man, I don't mean no disrespect, but thanks for saving my life, dawg," Shawn said.

"Don't thank me. Thank that big nigga there tying

those bean burrito eating muthafuckers up. And you need to thank your father most of all for never giving up on you. It's because of me that you're in here, but don't worry about that. Cash will pay, you can believe that! Let me see your phone, Country."

Pulling out of the storage lot, Kane stopped at the front window and gave the lady the key back and five thousand dollars to keep her mouth shut about this. Dialing Rooney's personal number made him upset to the point that he knew he had to get out before it came back to bite him. He knew about playing with snakes. Eventually, that snake would bite its owner. "Rooney, this is Kane. I don't mean to disturb you, Sir, but I need you to have José call me right away."

"Everything a'ight? Is there anything I can do?"

"Yeah. Just do what the fuck I asked you to do!"

"Kane—" The phone went dead before he could finish his statement. For Kane to talk like that, something had seriously gone wrong. Rooney did as he was asked.

Chapter 16

"Hola, papi! Como esta?"

"What's good, José?"

"Esta muy bien. Y tu?"

"Asi, asi."

"What's the problem, brother?"

"*Papi,* I got two of your goons down here. They've been cutting side deals with Cash, and if I'm not mistaken, they killed my little brother and were on their way to kill me. I need to know if you gave the order."

"*Papi,* I never would do anything of the sort! They acted on their own. But to show my gratitude, don't kill them. I'll be in the States by sunset tomorrow. Can you hold them for that long, or do you have a prior engagement to attend?"

"Well, let's just say that I have a little birdie to catch myself, so I'll see you tomorrow."

"Hasta luego, papi!"

José was the man behind Rooney, and Kane had

never seen him face to face. José knew Rooney was a slime bucket, but he needed his political connections to get the dope in and distributed in the States. Rooney was smart enough not to introduce the two. He knew that as soon as they met, he would be cut off. Rooney had no problem with them talking over the phone because there would be times that he would be gone and would not be able to be around to pick up or drop off, so he had no choice but to give Kane the link.

At first, Kane didn't give a damn, just as long as the dope didn't stop coming in. But as he got older, wiser and richer, he started thinking about cutting the middleman out. One thing Kane had learned from Rooney about the game was that there were no rules. It was every man for himself. As long as Kane could stay on top, he knew that one day, sooner or later, he and Rooney would clash.

José was a smart businessman. Rooney had served his purpose, and his services were no longer needed. José had become well connected with the same people that Rooney knew. But most importantly, so did Kane. Plus, José knew that Kane was the one moving all of the dope, so Rooney was a weak link and the easiest to be replaced.

After their conversation, José knew that it was time to meet the young man that has been making him money over the last ten years. He had been in the game a long time and had never seen a hustler such as Kane. What he saw in Kane was himself. He knew that Kane had ruled with an iron fist, but most of all, he respected him for his word. If Kane said something, you could write it in blood and take it to the bank.

Back at Bouncers, Cash was enjoying every second

of his life, not knowing that they were being counted down for him.

Kane and Country knew that they had to catch up with him before he disappeared again. Catching him at the club would be perfect. Kane knew that Cash couldn't be seen with the two Mexicans, so once he and Country walked in, he would be ready to disappear. Time was of the essence.

When Country pulled the Range into the parking lot, Carp and Kane stood outside for a second, contemplating their next move.

"Carp, I need a favor. I need you to hand out some flyers for the big police baller bash tomorrow night. I need you to make sure that all the names on this list are there, and that they believe that it's a surprise for the mayor. I'll bring him in myself. Can you handle that?"

"No question. Is there anything else?"

"Those two names, Mitch Crimson and Thomas Howe, make sure they are the first ones there. Other than that, get your son and go the hell home to your wife. But don't let the media know about him yet. Don't let him leave the house 'til this blows over. I'll call you."

Cash had just stepped out of the door to see Kane walking away from a black Lexus before it pulled out of the lot. "Who was dat, Kane?" he asked.

"That nigga, Black was trying to show me his new whip. Your boy is coming up in the game. You must be getting some bread off that side shit."

"Yeah, I'm seeing a little something. Anyway, what brings you out this way?"

"Me and Country were headed to the range to release some stress, then I saw your car and changed my mind. Why shoot a gun all day when I can come in here and bust a nut?"

"Kane, you're crazy as hell! But I'm 'bout to bounce."

"Damn, lil' bro! You can't hang with a nigga this morning? For real, I need you to come back in here and sit down for a minute. We've got something to discuss. We're about to handle some major shit. José is coming over tomorrow, and Rooney is about to retire from the game. That will put us all the way in, lil' bro."

At first Cash was upset for being in the damn club without his gun. But once Kane said what he said, he didn't care about anything but the streets and making money. Turning around and heading back into the club, he was still nervous about the two Mexicans showing up while he was with Kane, but he couldn't leave. He knew that he had to be with Kane and Country when they met José. Cash's mind was racing a hundred miles per hour. Watching his surroundings and the front door, he suggested that they head to a private room.

Kane had his eye on a piece already, but the time for her wasn't now.

After they entered the private room, E-Dubb came in with a couple of bottles of Ciroc. Once the door was shut, Country stood posted up by it to make sure that there would be no interruptions.

Opening his briefcase, Kane showed E-Dubb the blueprints to his new club, Shakers and Bouncers. E-Dubb didn't understand. "Kane, where are you opening this?"

"Right here. Let me explain. Remember what we talked about when we were at Edgefield?"

"Yeah, but what are you getting at? You gonna add to this joint?"

"Look. I'm gonna be straight with you. Me and Cash are hosting a big police baller bash here tomorrow. We're trying to get all the crooked bastards in here and blow their bitch asses to Kingdom Come. Once we knock Rooney off, we will own the city. Are you in? Before you answer, I've already gotten all the permits signed off for you. So, what do you think?"

"Nigga, I'm in! Just let me be the one to press the button!"

"Well, when you close tonight, Country will wire this whole muthafuckin' building to blow. I'll be here to make sure all the hoes get out safely. Make sure you put a sign outside that says it's closed for renovations. Ain't no need for no one to be here that ain't on the list. Get the DJ to leave a couple of mix CD's, and everything else is good."

On the couch, Kim was asleep in Kwantie's lap, while Kwantie was thinking about how Kim was watching Kane fuck her. She wasn't sure if Kim would fuck him if she had a chance. She really didn't care, but she wanted to know. Kwantie was willing to enjoy the both of them at the same time. She had the world in the palm of her hands. Her man was in the game and was about to get into politics. She had one of the baddest bitches eating her pussy, and the biggest nigga in town fucking her. She knew she would never have to work again a day in her life, especially if she could get both of them in the bed at the same time. She had feelings for Cash, but she knew that Cash would always be second to Kane. He wasn't a born leader. He would be nothing but a petty ass hustler who took orders from another nigga in charge. He had no balls. Plus, she knew the nigga was getting high on his own supply, but she never said anything to Kane.

But, the situation with Kim and Kane was eating at her. She was in love with both of them, and didn't want to make a choice. When this war was over in the streets, she didn't know what she was gonna do.

Looking down at Kim, she started running her fingers through her hair and kissing her on her forehead until she woke up. "Baby girl, I have something that I need to ask you."

"What is it, Kwantie?"

Chapter 17

"Cash, can I depend on you tomorrow night, man? 'Cause this will put us all the way in the game. Everything that we worked for has finally paid off."

"Cuzzo, have I ever let you down yet?"

"Country, you got everything to blow this joint straight to hell?"

"Boss man, you know it!"

"E-Dubb, get your beach towel and Mauri gator sandals. We're flying up out of here immediately as soon as it's done. Damn, Cash! What about Kwantie? You need me to send her a ticket, lil' bro?"

"Fuck that bitch! She wasn't shit anyway!"

"Well fellas, this will be our last meeting at Bouncers. The next time we meet, it will be Shakers and Bouncers."

Everyone lifted their glasses in unison and toasted before downing their drinks.

Kane really didn't want to let Cash out of his sight, but he had enough trust in him. When it came to killing cops, Cash would be the first in line, so he was the least of his worries.

Kane, Carp and Rooney had not heard a peep out of Mitch Crimson or Thomas Howe in the last couple of days. The two were incognito. They only seemed to pop up at the wrong time. Every time Kane would have someone tail them, they would shake them.

Kane had a plan with a deadline, and was not about to let anything or anybody get in his way. His dreams were becoming a reality. He had a few more kinks to work out, but other than that, he would be okay. He knew that before he could go away, he would have to get rid of the two undercover agents.

Right now, Carp was on his side, Cash was still unaware of Kim and Kwantie, and Rooney had no idea about José coming to the States. Tomorrow was a big day, and he needed to get some rest. He was not about to get caught slipping. He needed time to collect his thoughts.

Pulling out of the parking lot, Kane watched as Cash turned in the opposite direction, hoping he was not headed to the storage facility. He picked up his phone and dialed. "Lil' bro, where are you headed right now?"

"I'm headed to the crib. I need some rest, cuzzo. I've been ripping and running for the last couple of days. I just want to make sure I'm fresh. I'll hit you in the morning."

Kane covered his tracks. Even if Cash had gone to the storage, he had Carp place two squad cars on the back road to the building. They were ordered to pull him over for the slightest thing and lock him up. But nothing ever came of it.

Kane had made a U-turn and doubled back by Cash's

house just to make sure that he was really there.

Getting off the elevator, he didn't slip this time. He put his ear to the door before entering. All the lights were out except for the one coming from the television. He saw the two women lying on the couch, but wasn't sure of what he had seen. To him, Kim was lying with her head in Kwantie's lap. He thought he saw Kim slide her hand from underneath Kwantie's mini skirt and just blew it off.

He walked over and kissed Kwantie on her lips and asked Kim if she was doing better.

If only he knew how much better she really was! For real, she was doing better than he was! She was living the life. She was living with a man she wanted to fuck and who fantasized about fucking her while she was fucking his own lady. She wondered what would have happened if he walked in while they were doing their thing.

Kwantie had gotten up and made her way to the kitchen to fix his plate. "Baby, relax. Go take your shower and let me warm your food up."

"Kwantie, do you love me?"

"You know I do. What kind of question is that? You're making me nervous."

"Look. What I'm about to ask you, don't get mad, just be honest. Would you sleep with another woman for me?"

At first she thought he had caught them or had read her mind, but she didn't want to seem too eager to answer the question. "Where did that come from? Kane, I know you're out there fucking other bitches, but now you want to add me to your freaky shit? What, I'm not good enough for you? I'm not satisfying you by myself?"

"No, that's not it. I was at the club, and I was watching two chicks perform on each other and wondered what it would be like if I had that for myself, but both of the women must really love me."

"To be honest, if I found someone that we could both trust and knew was willing to be with both of us with no drama, I'd probably try it once for you just as long as you don't look at me different when we finish. But I'd never let two men do it to me in a threesome! Why? Who do you have in mind?"

He couldn't tell her about the chick in the club, and she couldn't say anything about Kim. Kim was lying on the couch smiling while Kwantie stood in the kitchen smiling. Kane walked down the hall, grinning from ear to ear, and thinking about Giovanni.

"Partner, wake up! Cash is on the move!"

"Well, follow his ass, Mitch. Stay on his ass. Where is Kane?"

"He's still parked in the back. Hold on, he's pulling off right now, but he's going the other way. Who do you want me to follow, Thomas?"

"Follow Cash. Kane ain't gonna get into much. That Cash, he keeps himself in shit. Ever since we saved his life, his ass hasn't been still. But if there's one thing I know, that nigga there will die in these streets, for the streets, and because of the streets."

"Thomas, you're crazy as hell, partner! But I know that until we get that money from his ass, I'm not letting him die anywhere in these streets unless it's from natural causes, and I might beg God Almighty to hold up on that!"

As the two agents followed Cash to his new crib, he was unaware of the company he had. He didn't give a damn about anything or anyone right now. Carp's son could have died in the storage room, Nut was dead, Kim was afraid to say a damn word, and Kwantie was just another piece of pussy that could be replaced. If Cash could kill Carp before they left, he would try. But what was more important right now was getting away with murder and everything that he had done in the streets.

Still not paying attention, Cash pulled into his driveway and parked. Before getting out of the car, he sat back and took a deep breath. A few minutes had passed before he finally got out and walked up his marble walkway.

Feeling a little paranoia set in as soon as he put his key in the door, he looked over his shoulder and noticed the black Yukon passing slowly by his house. Still peeking as he stepped through the door, he noticed the truck pull into a driveway a few houses down the road from him. As he waited for the occupants to get out, he was shocked when he saw the two white men get out and go into the house.

Cash knew that he had been tripping ever since the attempts on his life had been made. He had not been living in the neighborhood long enough to really know what cars belonged and which ones didn't.

Once in the house, he locked the door, set the alarm and rolled a blunt. Flopping down on the couch had caused him to relax a little. The blunt had gotten so good to him that he started thinking about some of the sexcapades that he and Nut had been in together. He began rubbing his dick while still smoking. The more he thought about it, the harder his erection became.

Knowing that he probably wouldn't enjoy another night like the ones he enjoyed with his road dawg, Nut, he called E-Dubb and had him send Lexus and Steph to his crib so he wouldn't be alone for the night.

Cash woke up from the sun peeking through his blinds. Looking at his watch, he just smiled. Waking between Lexus and Steph had made his day already. Then, being able to kill a couple of crooked cops would be the icing on the cake.

As he tried to slide out of bed, Lexus ducked down under the covers and put her lips on him and began her morning blowjob, while Steph licked him from the other side. He knew he was going to be occupied for a few more hours and didn't mind. This was a hell of a going away present he gave himself. To him, it wasn't tricking if you had it like that.

Before enjoying himself once again, he had set his watch to make sure that no matter what, he would be in the shower with them, so he could be up and out on the streets. He had a few loose ends he had to tie up. With Nut gone, he couldn't count on Country to collect his money. He knew that Country was too loyal to Kane to even fuck with him. Given a chance, he would blow Country's brains out of his skull.

Cash was sort of jealous of the two of them. At first he really liked Country, but then Nut was more on his level. He and Nut became so close that it made Kwantie upset.

Kwantie thought that something was wrong, so she hid a video camera in the house, hoping to catch them talking about other hoes so that she could flip on him and whip some bitch's ass.

A few weeks had gone by, and she finally checked the tape.

"Kane, wake up, baby. There's something I need to tell you. I've been holding this inside since yesterday, but you need to know," Kwantie said.

"Baby, what is it? You know I have a long day ahead of me. It better not be no bullshit."

"Kane, remember when I told you that Cash stopped sleeping with me all those months ago? I thought it was me. But I know the way that me and you sex each other on the regular, that it couldn't be me. As a matter of fact, I'm just gonna show you the DVD." As she got up and put the DVD in the player, she had tears in her eyes at first.

Kane saw that she was serious and began to pay attention to the TV. As his eyes began to focus, he saw Cash with his head laid back on the couch, and all you could hear was a slurping sound. The camera had a built in self-focus. The head was bobbing up and down while Cash was biting his lip. Kane looked a little closer to see the cornrows on the dark complexioned female. Then, trying to see her face a little better, he got a clear view of Nut's face. "What the fuck! This faggot ass mutherfucker! I'll kill him myself! My little cousin is gay?"

"That's not the end, baby."

"I can't stand to watch anymore of this shit! What else is on the DVD?"

"It recorded him talking to Nut about killing Jason. I just got the DVD the other night when I packed all my shit and came out here. I looked at it last night before you came in. That's why I didn't know how to respond to your question. I was afraid that you would do something to me for showing this to you."

"Kwantie, did Kim see this?"

"No, only me, and now you."

"Listen. Pack y'alls' shit. After José lands, we're flying to Puerto Rico with him for my birthday."

"JB's Butcher Shop."

"What's up, fam? It's your boy. Man, I need to holla at you. We're about to have a family reunion and I wanted to know if there are any specials."

"Homie, for you I'll cater the whole reunion for damn near next to nothing. All I need is your credit card number and the location where to deliver the goods."

"Well, later tonight at Bouncers. I would like to have everything set up and ready to go no later than 10:00 tonight."

"Okay, I'll see you tonight, Sir. Is there anything in particular that you would like served?"

"Yes. Being that it's a big police baller bash, do you still have those two pigs that were dropped off the other day? If so, just make some pigs in a blanket, because before the night is over, they will be roasted pigs!"

"A'ight! I feel you, dawg!"

"One last thing, JB. Bring your suntan lotion!"

"Mayor Rooney's office. May I ask who's calling?"

"Ma'am, please inform him that Mr. Woodson is on the line."

"Please hold."

"This is Rooney. What's good, Kane?"

"Well, I'm having a little birthday bash tonight, and I want you there. I also heard that I've been elected to a seat on the City Council, thanks to none other than my longtime friend."

"You know I wouldn't miss it for the world."

"Don't worry about the media or the paparazzi. I took it upon myself to rent the entire club out so we'll enjoy ourselves all night. I'm sending a personal Limo to pick you up at 10:00 this evening."

"Well, Mr. Woodson, I can't wait. It's been a while since we've been out to enjoy ourselves."

Chapter 18

Kane was busy trying to put everything into play. He didn't have time to allow anything to distract him. Calling everyone and setting the wheel in motion was his first priority. But he couldn't get what Carp said about his parents out of his mind. That alone was enough to drive him insane. Also, the fact that his cousin was gay was eating at him. His entire empire was crumbling right before his eyes. But because of his inner strength, he knew he had the power to prevail. He has been in the game since high school, and had only been to jail once, and that was to save Jason's ass.

Back in the day, Jason was about to receive a scholarship from the University of Clemson. Kane wanted his little brother to be something in life. He tried his best to keep him off the streets, but due to his time away in prison, Jason started hanging with Cash. Rooney had put both of them on his payroll without Kane's permission.

Jason caught a case while Kane was still in prison,

and Rooney had taken care of it and made it disappear. But, he made it clear that when the time came, Jason would have to pay the piper.

Rooney was a manipulative muthafucker. He would take control of anyone who was weak and turn them into a virtual modern day slave. But he had one problem: Kane and Country were different. The first time he saw them kill, he knew right then that he was going to have to play fair with them or end up dead.

Rooney saw weakness in Nut. Nut was the one getting high and was out in the streets trying to showboat. Kane and Big Country wouldn't smoke to save their lives while they were hustling. They weren't with the flamboyant shit. They were not into all of the sporty cars and jewelry. They always tried to keep a low profile. Out of sight, out of mind was their motto. But Nut always did the opposite.

While Kane was in prison, Cash and Jason had bonded, until Kane came back home. The streets hadn't changed much in the time that he was gone. It had only been nine months. But it did change enough for Cash and Jason to think that they were the next big kingpins.

What they didn't know or expect was for Kane to come home and still want to be the king. Kane had been in the game too long and had put in too much work in the streets just to lie down and take their shit.

Within those nine months, Cash and Jason rose quickly and were sitting on kilo money. They had become the two hottest hustlers in Anderson. They had all the women, the newest whips, and all the right connections.

No one knew how much time Kane had exactly, because he and Country kept it a secret. The entire time that Kane was gone, Country kept him informed on everything that was going on. When it came time for Kane to get out, Country was the one who picked him up from the prison.

Cash and Jason had gotten word from Rooney that Kane was being released. So, before Kane got home, they put together a surprise party for him to welcome him home. Kane and Country were surprised themselves when they got to the house. They couldn't figure out how anyone knew that Kane was out.

As everyone got their party on, he just sat back and watched everything and everybody.

From the corner where he was sitting, one particular female had grabbed his attention. As she walked through the crowd, he just watched her until her slanted eyes locked in with his, putting him in a daze. He snapped out of it when he saw Jason walk up and kiss her, and he knew he had to let her get away because of the love he had for his little brother.

As the party came to an end and everyone started leaving, Kane and Country made their way to the private room that Kane had built onto his parents' house. Country then went to find Nut, but came back without him. Jason came in by himself, and then a few minutes later Cash and Nut entered.

Once all of them were in the room, Kane began speaking. He let Cash and Jason know that their run was over, and they were going to have to fall in line and play their parts.

At first Cash had disagreed. Jason spoke up and wasn't with it either. Jason felt like he and Cash were the leaders of their own army, and they weren't about to step down for anyone.

Kane was not one to repeat himself, but because Jason was his brother, he tried to explain to him that what they were doing while he was locked up was a temporary thing, and now that he was back home, they would either get in line and follow his orders, or go against him.

Jason got up and walked out cursing.

Cash asked a few questions before leaving. He wanted to know if the prices would stay the same, and whether he and Jason could keep their same clientele. Kane had no problem with his demands. They shook hands and Cash left, trying to catch up with Jason.

After everyone was gone, Kane called Rooney to inform him that he was back and business would be back to normal within a few days.

After making further calls, the streets knew that he was back. Even though some of his people had gone to Cash and Jason, the older heads stayed loyal because of his political connects. They knew they were much safer dealing with Kane than with Cash and Jason. Cash and Jason had a long way to go in the game to get to the level that Kane was on.

Jason was upset. Instead of just playing his part, he went straight to Rooney and asked him what the hell was going on.

Talking to Rooney was like making a deal with the devil. Rooney explained to Jason that he had been dealing with Kane for too long to just cut him off. The two men had made millions together. But he also explained to Jason that there was always room to make improvements. He wanted to know how badly he wanted the number one spot.

Jason explained that it was his time to shine and time for Kane to step down.

Rooney looked at the young kid and smiled, because he saw Kane all over again. But he also knew that Jason wasn't mentally ready like Kane was.

Becoming frustrated, Jason asked Rooney what he would do if Kane just happened to die.

Rooney told him that if anything like that was to happen, then there would be an opening on his starting lineup.

Making his way to the door, Jason looked back at Rooney and told him that he would soon be on top, and that was his word. Before he got out the door, Rooney stopped him and explained the meaning of giving a man his word in the streets. Jason looked him in the eyes and repeated himself, then turned and walked out.

On the way home, Jason couldn't believe that he was having thoughts of killing his own brother; his own blood; his own flesh. But in the game, there was only one way to the top, and that was going through the man that was on top. He had convinced himself into believing that what he was about to do was going to happen anyway. Plus, he had always been in the background growing up in their parents' home.

He couldn't back down now. He had made a commitment and gave his word to Rooney, and now he had to prove his manhood. It was either kill his brother, or have Rooney kill him. That didn't take much of a thought. Kane had to go.

A couple of days had passed before he started coming back around. Cash didn't waste any time going back to hustling under Kane's orders. When Jason told Cash that he wasn't bowing down to anyone, Cash explained to him that nothing had changed. The streets would still respect them and love them the same. They had the best of both worlds. But Jason couldn't see it.

Kane didn't trust his brother anymore. He saw the greed and envy in his eyes. So, when Jason called to set up a meeting, Kane told him that he would only meet him at their parents' house. Jason agreed to this.

It didn't take long for Jason to get there. When he pulled up, he saw Kane's 600 Benz parked in the garage.

Sitting in the house, Kane watched as Jason pulled up in the driveway. He went back into the living room to speak with his father before Jason made his way into the house.

It had been a while before Jason finally entered the house. When he did, he went straight to the bathroom, flushed the toilet and turned the water on and washed his hands. When he came out of the bathroom, he joined his brother and father in the living room, and all three men sat and talked about what was going on.

Listening to their father, it didn't take long before they came to an agreement, put the past behind them and let the beef go.

Jason agreed to play his part as long as he could get the same deal that Cash was getting. Kane had no problem with it, and even gave him a better deal. He would give the dope to Jason for the same price that he was getting it for. He shook Kane's hand, even though he didn't really care about the deal.

Before leaving, Jason went to the back to speak to his mother. Peeking into her room thinking she might be taking a nap, he saw her dressed in a black evening gown. That's when he realized that the reason his father was dressed up was because it was their 50th wedding anniversary, and every year they would go out or Kane would fly them somewhere special. Stepping into the room, he let his mother know how gorgeous she looked, and he gave her a couple of stacks and told her to enjoy themselves.

Walking out of the house, he looked at the 600 Benz

one more time and smiled. As he was getting into his car, Cash's parents pulled up, dressed to impress. Jason just beeped his horn and waved at them as he made his way down the driveway.

Back in the house, Kane watched his mother and father as they embraced and took pictures as if this was their prom night all over again. When Cash's parents came in also dressed up, Kane couldn't do anything but smile, because he knew where he had gotten his swag from. His father and uncle had run Anderson back in the heroin days and were able to retire from the game. Now all they did was sit back and enjoy life.

Before leaving, Kane tossed the keys to his 600 Benz to his father and took their Cadillac for the weekend.

Chapter 19

"Kane, where are you? I have those papers for you. You need to see this."

"A'ight, meet me at Capri's on Clemson Boulevard in ten minutes."

"Sure. I'll be there with the quickness. I'm coming through the east side right now. Oh yeah, I just saw Cash with two chicks in his car over there."

"A'ight, Carp. If you get there before I do, give the hostess my name and she'll seat you."

"Kim, wake up, baby and get dressed. We're 'bout to go on a shopping spree. Kane called and said that we're going to fly over to Puerto Rico tonight, girl. You know we got to be the flyest bitches that they ever seen when we get there. Oh yeah, I forgot to tell you that it's Kane's birthday in two days."

"Oh yeah? Well, what can you possibly get a nigga that has everything already?"

"Shit if I know! I know one thing he hasn't got—or should I say two?"

"Have you asked him yet, Kwantie?"

"No, but you heard what he said to me in the kitchen."

"I don't think he was talking about us. I think he was talking about one of them chicks from the club."

"We'll see about that!"

"Welcome to Capri's. Would you like smoking or non smoking?"

"Hello, ma'am. I'm here to meet a Mr. Woodson."

"Right this way, Sir."

Reaching the back of the restaurant, Carp reached over and shook Kane's hand, and then handed him a manila envelope before sitting down.

Kane didn't waste any time opening it. "Carp, what is this?"

"It's a CD recording of a conversation."

"Oh yeah? How do I know you ain't recording us right now?"

"You don't. But to be honest, I was recording you in the beginning of my investigation, but once you gave me my son back, I destroyed all of the evidence I had on you. But you need to listen to this CD as soon as possible. As for tonight, my part of the deal is done. Anything else? If not, I'll see you tonight."

"Well Carp, there is one last thing I'm gonna need before this is done. I'm gonna need your son to go to Carolina's Luxury Limo Service. Instructions will be left there for him. Other than that, I really appreciate everything that you have done for me."

"You're welcome, Kane. Take care of that Kim. As far as me and you, if you come back to Anderson, South Carolina, I'll catch you later."

As both of the men got up and walked out of the restaurant, they said their good byes and parted.

Kane went straight to his truck and put the CD in. When it first came on it was hard to understand what was being said. The sound was distorted, but as it continued playing it began to clear up. The more he listened, the more he was able to distinguish the different voices.

Hearing Jason's voice plotting on his life with Rooney was a hard pill to swallow. His little brother wanted to kill him. He couldn't believe that Rooney had turned his brother against him.

Kane's eyes watered and tears began to run down his face. His eyes had changed to bloodshot red. With his light complexion, he was sitting in his truck looking like a demon. With his dreads hanging over his face, he had become a possessed animal. Nothing was what it seemed right now.

As the CD continued to play, Kane pulled out the of the photos that were in the envelope. The first one was of his 600 Benz. As he kept looking through the pictures, he stopped when he got to the one with his break line dangling from under his car. In the next picture were fingerprints that the police had recovered off of the break line. What Kane saw had shocked him. Jason had really tried to kill him, but ended up killing their parents and their aunt and uncle. Everything began to make sense now.

As Kane sat in the truck, he started replaying in his mind what really happened the day that he gave his parents his Benz. At first it didn't come to him, but the longer he sat there and thought about it, the more it became clearer.

That day will always be stuck in his mind. He would always remember that as they pulled out of the driveway, he followed them down the street to the highway where he turned off, and they kept going, heading to the highway. The highway was less than a mile from their house so they had made it there before the brake fluid had run out.

They were doing about 75 miles per hour, and were unable to stop the car. When the brakes failed, it had caused them to slam into the back of an 18-wheeler. There was also another truck right behind them traveling at the same speed.

The report that Carp gave Kane had broken him down completely. Unable to drive, he sat in his truck for a few minutes before he reached over, grabbed his 50 cal and aimed it at his temple.

"E-Dubb, what's going on, man? Has anybody heard from Kane yet?"

"Nah, Big Country. I figured he would have called or at least came through by now. You don't think anything's happened to him, do you?"

"Man, we done came too far for anything to happen now. He's probably tying up a bunch of loose ends. We can't be thinking like that."

"I feel you. But that nigga, Cash is a different story. That nigga is a real slime bucket."

"Yo, E-Dubb, make a few calls and see if anyone has heard anything. I'm gonna hit the strip and see what I can find out."

"Shit, here comes Cash now! I forgot that he was with Lexus and Steph all night."

"What's up, my niggas? Why y'alls' faces all down

and gloomy? Shit, we need to be smiling. We 'bout to be on top of the world. Better than that, we 'bout to own a piece of the world. Where da fuck is Kane at?"

"That's what we're trying to figure out. We thought you might've heard something."

"Me? You big cornbread eating ass nigga! It's your fucking job to watch that nigga. I swear, if anything has happened to my cousin—my flesh and blood—I'll kill every muthafuckin' bastard walking the face of this green Earth, starting with you two!"

"Cash, everybody's upset, but if you ever threaten me again, I won't wait to hear from Kane. I'll kill you right on the spot where your ass stands!"

"Guys, come on! Man, this ain't the time for that." E-Dubb couldn't stop the two men from arguing before Cash pulled his gun out.

Still sitting in the truck, Kane continued to blame himself for his parents' death. Then, a voice on the CD interrupted his thoughts. Carp was speaking:

> *"Kane, if you are still listening to this CD, that means you are a strong man. I wanted to thank you again for saving my son's life and getting him back to me alive."*
>
> *"I had a few of my trusty friends run a thorough investigation on the car, and these were the results: It was no accident, as you can see. Jason had tampered with the break line. I apologize to you for having to find out this way."*
>
> *"As far as Cash, I'll leave him to you. I had his house bugged"*
>
> *"Rooney was the only other person alive with*

this information. He played Cash against Jason, and Jason against you, and now he's promised Cash your empire if he gets rid of you. See, Rooney gave Cash this same information about y'alls' parents, but Cash didn't have enough heart to kill Jason."

"Now, that's where the two white undercover agents come into play. Cash offered them a substantial amount of money, and couldn't come up with it due to you putting a hold on their hustling. He'd been trying to cut side deals, but no one in the surrounding counties would fuck with him because of you. Once the police killed Jason, he thought everything would go back to normal and you would put him in charge of Jason's spot. But you didn't. You put Kim in the spot."

"Rooney had told him about the prices that you were giving Jason the dope for, and he figured with Jason gone he would be able to build up his clientele, and then eventually take you out."

"Everything that Kim told you about the murder was right. She didn't hold anything back."

"Jason had told Cash about you and Kwantie. He just could never catch y'all two in the act. Even though Cash really didn't give a fuck, he still wanted to see harm come your way. Cash had someone else in his house satisfying his needs whenever Kwantie wasn't home. The mic we had installed in their house couldn't pick up the female's voice, but we could tell that whoever it was went straight to work and would leave as soon as they were done."

"Kane, when you gave Kim Jason's portion, Cash couldn't take it. He felt that he had to kill her and you. Now, my question is, why didn't he kill her the night he raped her? We may never know the answer to that one, will we?"

"Make sure you are careful tonight. You don't know if Cash went to Rooney or not, but as far as the wiretaps, one is still in Cash's house. Until this morning, he hasn't made any comments or calls to anyone. I can tell you that he did have two females over last night, and they were still there when I left."

"As far as your information, let's just say my computer was lost in a fire and the rest was destroyed. You have my word. Everything in your hands as of right now is all that's left."

"Well, until tonight. I'm gone, and may God be with us!"

Still sitting in the truck, Kane ignored his phone. He dried his eyes, un-cocked his 50 cal and headed over to the club.

"Girl, you like this? It don't make me look too nasty, does it?"

"Kwantie, you know nothing can make you look nasty. You're already nasty!"

"Stop playing, Kim! Do you like it or what?"

"Yes, girl. With all of them thongs you're buying, you must know Victoria's Secret already!"

"I do! It's called 'Po-nanny'!"

"Girl, you are crazy as hell!"

As they finished shopping and were leaving the store, Kim stopped in her tracks when she looked through the window and saw Cash's BMW go by. They ran outside and jumped into the truck and tried to follow him, but they lost him.

"Damn! I lost him, girl! Oh well! What do you feel

like doing until later?"

Kwantie smiled, told her to pull over, and took her to Pandora's Box.

"What kind of place is this, Kwantie?"

"What do you think it is? We can't finger ourselves forever, so we might as well get some toys."

Kim had never imagined herself standing in an adult store picking out toys with another female who would be using them on her.

Kwantie let Kim pick out every item—from a double-headed dildo to anal beads. Kim had even picked out a few sexy negligees. She had other plans behind her actions. She wanted to impress Kane, and please Kwantie as much as she could. She was about to take flirting and freaking to a whole new level.

Chapter 20

"Nigga, after this shit is over, I'm gonna knock your big ass out! E-Dubb, I'm out! Call me if Kane gets in contact with you."

"Cash, hold up man! Where the fuck are you going? You know we only have a few hours, and it's already 5:30. We're supposed to meet up at 7:00, right?"

"Man, I got a couple of niggas that owe me. If Kane calls, just tell him that I'll be right back."

"Got-damn! Y'all niggas are always going at it. Y'all just need to put the guns down and fight like two men."

"E-Dubb, mind your business! This shit is bigger than that. That nigga is a punk!"

"Fuck you mean?"

"Nigga, did I stutter? He's a punk; gay; a muthafuckin' homo! Them bitches you got up in your club, you better have their asses checked out."

"Stop playin', dawg. I know you're pissed off, but damn! You don't have to slander the nigga's name like that."

"Look, man. At first I thought they had some shit going on the side, but one night while I was creeping, I had switched cars and was at the hotel up on Clemson Boulevard. I looked out the window and saw Nut's car pull into the parking lot. The shorty I was with had passed out and didn't like me smoking around her, so I went outside and sat in the car and rolled a blunt and smoked it to the head."

"I sat out there all fucking night. Before the sun came up, Cash came out of the same room that Nut had gone in. At first it didn't dawn on me, but when Nut came out after that, I was expecting to see two women, or at least one come out behind them, but nothing and nobody."

"Once they both pulled off, I saw an old Spanish lady doing housekeeping, and I offered her a couple of dollars to open the door for me. At first she knocked, but no one answered. That's when she opened the door. I thought I might find two females still in the room—or at least one like I said—but all I saw was two beds, and only one of them was messed up. Now, you tell me!"

They didn't notice Kane walking up. "Tell you what, Country?"

As Country began to explain, Kane hushed him and let him know that he already knew, and E-Dubb couldn't believe what the fuck he was hearing.

The buzzer to the back door sounded, and they looked at the TV monitor. JB was out back and ready to set up.

Kane went to the bar and grabbed a bottle of Ciroc for himself.

While JB was setting out the food, E-Dubb picked up one of the snacks, ready to eat it. JB couldn't help laughing, but stopped him before he bit into it.

"What's wrong with it, JB?"

"Man, let's just say that those two cops that were never found... well, you just found them!"

"Got-damn it, JB! You're always with that bullshit! I should've known not to eat anything that you bring to a police bash. I'm slippin'!"

"E-Dubb, if I didn't fuck with you, I would've let you eat that shit. But you my man, fifty grand!"

"I feel you, cuz. On the real though, JB, doesn't it feel good to be getting money and have no worries?"

"Hell yeah! Think about it, E-Dubb. If you wasn't fucking with us, your ass would still be working as a fucking C.O. What you make in one week at your strip club, it would take you two years to make working for the feds. Plus, look at the benefits. The feds don't fly you to Puerto Rico for an all expense paid vacation."

"You're right. Tonight needs to hurry the fuck up so we can get the fuck outta here!"

Cash was on the west side, collecting the money that was owed to him before Jason was killed. The last couple of weeks had been very hectic. He knew that if he didn't go collect it, niggas would start to get amnesia quickly and would not want to pay. But what Cash didn't know was that the Mexicans had put a small bounty on his head.

While he was on the west side waiting for Lil' Dirty to bring him his money, he opened a cigar and rolled up a blunt of purple haze. Sitting on the side of the crack house that he used to hustle out of, he was watching a young girl who was thick to death walking in front of his BMW and chewing bubble gum. With his attention on the girl, he didn't see Lil' Dirty creeping down the alleyway. By the time he noticed him, Lil' Dirty was already pulling a gun out of his waistband.

Cash was caught off guard and dropped his blunt. He was no stranger to a gunfight, but he had to get the fuck out of there. He put the car in drive and hit the gas in an effort to get out of the alleyway.

Lil' Dirty had gotten off three quick shots that shattered the back seat window on the driver's side.

Cash crashed into an old truck that was parked in front of the house as he tried to avoid hitting the young chick with the bubble gum. His air bag had deployed upon impact, and this caused him to be dazed for a second, until he saw that Lil' Dirty was still coming for him.

Opening his door, Cash crawled out onto the ground through the passenger side. The first couple of shots had just missed him by inches. Looking under the car, he wanted to see if all the practice at Better Aiming Shooting Gallery had paid off.

He lay down on the ground, pointed his Glock 40 with the infrared beam at the kid's ankle and fired. Watching the kid fall, he jumped up and ran over to him, kicked his gun away and stood over him with a devilish grin before putting two slugs into the kid's chest.

The screams from the young chick with the bubble gum made him run and jump back into his car. He then put the car in drive and pulled off.

While looking up the street, he saw the chick with the bubble gum holding a gun and walking down the middle of the street while firing straight into his windshield. Cash pressed the gas and picked up speed. As she kept shooting, he kept coming. Her gun had stopped firing, but it was too late. Cash was already up on her doing about 60 miles per hour. He felt the impact when she slammed into the car. She had hit the car so hard that her head cracked the windshield and blood covered the entire window.

Before he knew it, other gunshots began zooming over his head. He turned on the wipers and tried to get the hell out of the neighborhood as fast as he could.

The young chick's body was stuck on the car, and he was trying to reach out of the window to pull her off the hood. When he saw that he couldn't pull her off, he did the next best thing: he slammed on the brakes which caused the car to throw her lifeless body into the street. He then hit the gas and peeled off.

His adrenaline was pumping so much that he hadn't noticed that he was hit. Looking in the mirror, he started yelling. "Fuck! Who do they think they are, trying me, the muthafuckin' Prince of the City! Bitch, I'm Cashmere Woodson! I can't die! Fuck ass niggas, try again!" He continued to yell at the top of his lungs all the way back to the club.

He had to call Kane. He knew he was already running late and wasn't trying to mess anything up. He knew Kane was depending on him tonight. Before making the call, he reached into his pocket, pulled a bag of cocaine out and began snorting.

After returning the bag of coke to his pocket, with one hand on the steering wheel, he pressed the seven digits with his free hand. "Yo Kane, man, I'm hit! I just got shot, but I got away though. I went to pick up some money from them niggas on the west side, and one of them young niggas tried to rob me!"

"Cash, are you a'ight? Are you gonna make it, or do I have to meet you?"

"Nah, I'm good, cuz. I'll be there in about ten minutes. Where are you?"

"I'm here at the club. Hurry your ass up."

Kane did not like this at all. One of the stories he heard from all of the old school cats was that everything that's good will come to an end, and it usually comes when you're trying to get out of the game.

This was just another sign that he had to hurry up and meet with José and get the hell out of the States for a little while. Shit was starting to get thick, and he knew he had come too far to go out as a loser. Time was of the essence, and no matter what, Kane was not about to let Cash or Rooney mess up his plans.

As Cash hung up the phone, he knew he was quickly losing a lot of blood, and that he was probably still alive because of all the drugs he was taking. He wasn't stopping for any stop signs or red lights. He was on a mission to get to the club, dead or alive. If nothing else, he knew he didn't want to die alone in his car.

"Country, Cash just got shot. Go outside and wait for his stupid ass. This dumb ass nigga is gonna fuck around and get himself killed before I can kill him myself."

"Kane, no disrespect, homie, but send that nigga, E-Dubb out there. I might kill that nigga myself, boss man."

"You're right. I need you in here making sure that no one is in here snooping around. As a matter of fact, I'm gonna have Doc come over here and try to save that dumb ass nigga 'til we kill him."

"Kane, after this is over, man, I'm trying to get the fuck outta here, my nigga."

"Don't worry, my nigga. We're up outta here tonight. But right now, I'm gonna go pick that sorry ass excuse of a mayor up. Hold this shit together 'til I get back."

Chapter 21

"Kim, do you like this color? I think it's too big myself."

"Girl, we ain't doing nothing but renting it anyway. What did Kane say?"

"He said to get a black Excursion and be parked outside of the club no later than 10:00."

"Well, we don't have that much time left. What are we gonna do until then?"

"You hungry? We can go get something to eat if you want."

"I got something for you to eat, Kwantie!"

"What're you saying? You don't think I'll eat you right here?"

"I know you will. That's not the problem though. I'm trying to figure out why those two white men in that black Yukon have been watching us for the last few minutes."

"Kim, baby, you're just paranoid. They ain't watching us. They look like they're smoking a blunt or something.

But if they are watching us, I don't have a problem with giving them something to look at!"

As Kim parted her legs to let Kwantie go face first between her thighs, she laid her head back so that she could enjoy her tongue. Opening her eyes every few seconds to see if anyone was looking, she noticed the two white men climb out of their truck and walk right past them.

Kim's breathing had picked up the faster Kwantie licked and nibbled on her lips. She arched her back to let Kwantie slide two fingers up in her.

Biting on her bottom lip, Kim never took her eyes off of the two white men. Watching them, she noticed the smaller of the two and the way he was standing. She wasn't sure what was going on. All of the sudden she saw the walkie-talkie come out of his pocket and go up to his mouth. Then she saw them turn around and run back to their truck, jump in and turn their red and blue lights on. As soon as she saw this, her heart froze with fear. She had to cover her mouth to stop from screaming out aloud.

The muffled sound made Kwantie think that she was the cause of the loud moan.

Once they were in the truck and had pulled off, Kim had let out the scream.

"Damn, bitch! Is it that good?"

"No… I mean yeah… no! No, Kwantie! Those two white men in the truck..."

"What about them? Baby, tell me something. You're starting to scare me."

"I'm sorry, Kwantie, but they're police. Those were the same two who came to my house the night that Jason was murdered."

"And? Why're you acting like they were trying to kill you?"

"That's just it, Kwantie! They were the same two

who came in and robbed us and killed Jason! Then, they came to the house later in their regular clothes. There was something that made me nervous and my stomach twitch. And even though my gut was telling me something different, I ignored it because the rest of the police force knew them. I told Carp, but I don't know if he ever checked it out. Kwantie, we need to call Kane and let him know."

Pulling up at Rooney's crib, Kane made sure that his vest was extra tight and his gun was locked and loaded with one in the chamber. The Limo driver had gotten out and waited for Rooney to exit the house. Kane was getting nervous, but then he saw Rooney coming out of the door. Kissing his wife goodbye made Kane smile because he knew that it would be his last kiss.

Before Rooney entered the Limo, following Kane's orders, the driver searched him, taking all precautions. "I see you haven't changed, Kane."

"I see you haven't changed either. He will keep the gun up front with him until the night is over. Other than that, what the fuck took you so long? I was about to leave your ass and go party by myself."

"Partner, I didn't mean to be late, but some crazy muthafucka got into a shootout over there on the west side."

"Anybody hurt?"

"Well, they told me that some dirty little kid got shot twice in his chest. They say a man got out of a car and walked right up on him and shot him. Then his sister was running down the street to help him, and the driver of the car ran her over."

"Damn! Whoever that nigga was, he was crazy as hell! Did they catch him yet?"

"No. You know the streets won't talk. They'll contact you about it before me, Mr. City Councilman!"

"Yeah, that does sound good, doesn't it? You know what's after that, right?"

"What, Mr. Woodson?"

"Mayor!"

"That's what I love about you, Kane. You are so persistent."

"But enough about that. Let's enjoy tonight. You know what they say: 'All work and no play makes for a dull day'!"

Pulling into the parking lot of the club, Cash was in and out of consciousness. Barely able to get out of the car, he slammed the car in park and fell out of the door.

E-Dubb and Doc ran over and carried him through the back door, where Doc had one of the private rooms already set up to operate on Cash.

Looking at the wound, Doc really didn't have much work to do. The bullet went through Cash's shoulder, but he had lost a lot of blood, which was causing his weakness. Sewing his shoulder up didn't take as long as he thought it would.

E-Dubb paid Doc like Kane told him to and showed him out of the back door.

Country had moved Cash's car around to the back and armed it with a couple of sticks of C-4 explosives. Country meant business tonight.

"Kwantie, what's going on, baby? There's been a change of plans. Did you get the truck yet…? Well, meet me at the club ASAP. Park in the front and get into the Limo that's parked outside."

"Kane, Kim needs to talk to you."

"About what? Can't it wait?"

"No. You need to hear this right now."

"Well, put her on the phone."

"Kane, those two cops in the pictures, they're the ones who came in the house and robbed us! They killed Jason! I just saw them, and it came to me. I remembered every little movement they made. You taught me to trust my gut instincts, so believe me."

"Baby girl, don't worry, I know. We'll handle that like I promised. Right now, I'm with a client."

"Kane, are those the hoes for the night? Man, it's been so long since I've had some black meat," Rooney said.

"Well, Rooney, that's your fault for marrying a white woman. Then, you hired one as your secretary. But she is fine though. Plus, the pussy is good!"

"What the hell do you mean?"

"Your secretary, Rooney. Who do you think is hitting that thing when you ain't home?"

"Kane, like I said, you never cease to amaze me. That 'I don't give a fuck' attitude will take you far in politics. But the first day you bring your feelings to work, it's over. I knew from that day with Country's uncle that you were going far. And, you kept your childhood friend with you."

"Well, Rooney, I look at life like this: It's better to have people love to hate you, than never having had love at all. Feel me?"

While sitting in front of the club, Rooney noticed a lot of white undercover cops going into the club, but he paid it no mind. When the Excursion pulled up and he saw the two beautiful black women step out of the truck, he shifted in his seat and grabbed his crotch.

When Kwantie opened the door and got in, she leaned over, exposing her thong long enough for Rooney to get a peek. Kissing Kane on the lips and sitting on his lap let Rooney know that she was taken.

As Kim got out of the Excursion, Kane smirked while looking at her. She was dressed identical to Kwantie, all the way down to her thong, which she let Rooney get a sneak peek at while getting situated on the seat beside Kane. Once comfortable, she leaned over and kissed him on the cheek. After the introductions, everyone enjoyed a glass of Ciroc and brief conversation.

Kane stepped out of the Limo and left the girls there with the mayor. Back in the club, he was greeted by Obsession. Stopping in his tracks, he asked whether she was busy tonight, and she told him that he would be seeing her before he left.

Heading to the back, he went in and saw Cash sprawled out on the floor, knocked out. Doc had given him the sedative that was ordered.

"Country, I need you to go outside to the Limo and get the keys to the rental from Kwantie and pull it around back. Then put this bum ass nigga in there. JB, take

E-Dubb's gun and stay in the truck with Cash. If he wakes up, put his ass back to sleep. E-Dubb, I need you to go out and mingle with the guests. Make sure them hoes are putting in work. I want those bastards to smile before they die."

Sitting in the Limo, the girls were holding small talk with the mayor, and could see the lust in his eyes. They would periodically open and close their legs, which distracted him so much that he hadn't noticed how much time had gone by.

After Country came and got the keys, the doors were locked and the driver was given strict orders from Kwantie to tap on the door if anyone else came towards the car.

The mayor loosened his tie once the girls started teasing him. Kwantie had opened her legs wide enough for him to see her lips hugging the front of her thong. Then, Kim leaned over and started to lick on Kwantie's neck until her nipples hardened. Almost drooling from the mouth, the mayor just stared at them.

Kwantie started rubbing on Kim's breasts until her nipples hardened. Lifting her shirt enough to expose her own breasts, Kwantie laid back and threw her leg over the back seat while Kim went down on her. Pouring Ciroc over her, she began to suck eagerly and slid the tip of the Ciroc bottle between Kwantie's legs, pushing it in and out. She took the bottle and handed it to the mayor and told him to taste the juices.

Rooney did what they said without hesitation.

Kim took it a step further and pulled the mayor's dick out and held it in her hand while she stared him in the eyes. Squeezing as hard as she could, Rooney stared back at her while he licked Kwantie's juices off of the bottle. Stroking his penis and his ego caused the mayor to ooze cum in her hand.

Letting him go, she backed away while Kwantie sat on top of him and grinded in his lap and let him squeeze her breasts. This had him feeling like he was in heaven. Grinding back and forth on his lap had caused her to get a little moist.

While the mayor's attention was focused on Kwantie, Kim poured him a glass of Ciroc, with a little something extra added to it. He was so distracted by Kwantie that he just took the glass and downed the drink in one gulp.

The mayor had never experienced anything like this. He was willing to do anything. While licking his lips, he leaned over to try to kiss Kim, and Kwantie slapped him and pushed him back in his seat. She took his necktie off and ripped his shirt off, popping all of the buttons.

The mayor was overwhelmed by their actions, and before he knew what was happening, he was naked and tied up at his wrists and ankles.

Kim and Kwantie straightened their clothes up and sat back as they watched the mayor's eyes slowly close.

Chapter 22

"Kane, E-Dubb told me to tell you that you have an important phone call."

"Did he say who it was, Giovanni?"

"He said to tell you it's José."

Rushing back to the office, he had been anticipating this call all day. "*Hola,* José!"

"Hey, bro! Is everything still the same?"

"*Si, papi.* Are you here yet?"

"Yes. Where do you want to meet?"

"The storage building by the airport in about a half hour."

"Okay. See you there."

Kane knew that it was time to put everything into effect, so he called everybody to the back and made the announcement. "Country, you and E-Dubb are going to be the last two to leave. Make sure that the building is clear of our people. E-Dubb, I need you to go out front and bring Giovanni, Lexus, Steph and two more chicks; one for Country and one for JB. Go ahead and put them in the Excursion and y'all meet me at the storage building. Don't stop for anything. We have twenty minutes to get there."

Kane went out to the DJ booth and ordered all the women to the back and turned the lights down. He then told the partying cops to gather around the stage and get their money ready because the show was about to begin. He fixed the CD to continue playing before headed out of the door.

All the strippers were getting in their cars and getting the hell out of the parking lot.

Country got in the truck and gave Kane the thumbs-up sign and pulled up to the Limo.

Checking the front door one last time, Kane saw the chain wrapped and padlocked around the handles and looked back at Country and nodded his approval. He then got into the Limo and they pulled off. He couldn't do anything but smile. The mayor was stretched out on the floor, butt naked. Before he could ask, Kwantie told him that it was too easy. He still had to ask though.

Kim laughed and told him that when Country came and got the keys, he handed her a pill and told her to put it in the mayor's drink.

Kane sat back and laughed while Kwantie sat in his lap.

"Got-damn! Where the fuck are the hoes at, man? Shit! I could have stayed at home with my fat ass wife!"

The officers had started getting restless. The CD was playing Drake and Lil' Wayne's, "I Wish I Could Fuck Every Girl in the World".

Then, Kane's voice came on, telling them that their

lives were about to be over. The devil had pulled all of their numbers out of the pit of hell tonight, and it was time for them to meet their Maker.

Smoke began coming out of the speakers and from under the stage. At first everyone thought the show was about to start, until the entire club became smoky. They rushed to the door to try to escape, but they were locked in from the outside. Realizing that no one had a gun, they started panicking. Trampling over each other trying to get out of the front door didn't help the situation in any way. Suddenly, all of the lights went out and it was pitch black. They never would have guessed that the club's gas line had been cut when they reached in their pockets and flicked on their lighters.

"Damn, Mitch! Did you see that? I wonder what the fuck that was."

"I don't know, Thomas, but whatever it was, it just lit up the whole city. Hey, Carp, what the fuck was that?"

Carp hid a smirk from them when he noticed the huge fireball roar into the night sky. "Hell if I know! I'm here with you two, looking at these two dead kids."

Fire truck sirens came to life and sounded in every direction. The walkie-talkies of every officer standing around came to life. The dispatcher was calling every available officer on and off duty to respond.

As soon as she gave the location, Mitch and Thomas looked at each other and were shocked. They knew immediately what was going on. The Woodson boys had struck again. Kane had put his foot down and struck the first blow.

Carp had no way of getting in contact with Kane at

the present time to inform him that the two agents were still alive. Carp was the one who had tried to get them to go to the baller bash.

Thomas looked over at Carp and noticed that he was pretending to look preoccupied. Thinking back, he remembered that Carp was the one who had given him and his partner the flyer and the VIP tickets to the bash. Carp had never been a party type of dude, but the more Thomas thought about the situation, he began to put the pieces of the puzzle together. Now it was making sense why Carp had insisted that he and Mitch attend the baller bash. "Mitch, let's go. That call is ours. That's the big police baller bash. I think it was a setup."

"What? Hell no, Thomas! You mean you think Kane would try some shit like that?"

"With a little help, hell yeah! Let's go. We'll get with his ass later. Aye Carp, you going to that call?"

"Yeah, I'm right behind y'all."

On the highway, E-Dubb pulled out his phone and dialed a number. When he hit the last button, everyone saw Bouncers go up in a ball of fire like it was Hiroshima.

In the Limo, Kane watched the fireball go up into the sky, and turned his head back around.

Kim and Kwantie didn't even ask. They continued sipping their drinks.

Back in the truck, Cash was just waking up. Seeing Lexus and Steph made him think that he was in heaven. But the pain in his left shoulder was so excruciating that he asked JB to roll a blunt for him.

Any other time JB would not have had a problem, but tonight he was under orders from Kane, and everyone knew Kane's policy about getting high when you're doing business for him.

Cash was used to having his way so much that he became hostile. The gun in JB's hand caused him to receive another small, temporary concussion.

Time was moving, and so were they. Kane always knew that being early was better than being late with a man like José. A good first impression would be best, and he would come correctly.

José also made plans for Kane and his crew to fly out to Puerto Rico for an unexpected vacation.

Pulling off the highway, they made the first right and were at the storage facility. Pulling into the parking lot, Kane saw the black Rolls Royce Phantom parked at the entrance. He got out and met José in the middle of the lot, assuring him that everything was straight.

Once José felt that everything was good, they proceeded with their business.

Kane lifted his hand, and JB got out with Cash over his shoulder. Country got out of the truck with E-Dubb and opened the gate to the storage building.

José watched the way Kane carried himself and gave orders without even having to speak. He was impressed.

Walking back to the Limo, JB opened the door and dropped Cash's body inside, stepped back out and ordered the driver to proceed to bin 229.

José and Kane walked behind the Limo, getting acquainted. They had only spoken over the phone. Now that they were face to face, the men were satisfied with their decision to meet in person.

Chapter 23

Lying in the Limo, the pills started wearing off. Rooney was beginning to open his eyes. Still in shock, he couldn't figure out what was going on. He had been tricked by some tricks. Nervously staring at the two women, he felt the Limo come to a stop. He was trying to focus his eyes when he began to wonder about where Kane was. His mind started racing. He was wondering if they had already gotten him, or if Kane was the one behind this. He was so scared that he didn't know what to think at that point.

Rolling over, he noticed another body behind his. It was Cash. His mind went into overdrive. If he could only get a glimpse of who else was in the Limo, it would shed some light on the situation.

He wanted to know who had enough balls and power to even attempt to try some shit like this. Seeing shadows outside of the window, he knew whoever it was, was outside of the car and he would be meeting them in a few minutes.

Kim noticed that he was straining to hear the voices outside, and turned the volume up on the CD player.

Twisting and turning, he was trying to loosen the rope that they tied his arms with, but the more he moved, the tighter the rope got.

Yelling at the top of his lungs only made matters worse. Kim kicked him in the face and told him to be quiet. "That was for Jason, you bastard!"

Trying to shake the cobwebs off, he spit the blood from his mouth where she had busted his lip directly at her.

Kwantie started laughing at him, which caused him to turn fire truck red. "You stupid ass cracker! You thought you were really finna get to taste some of this, didn't you? You white muthafuckas will do anything to taste some sweet chocolate. I see ain't nothing changed since the slavery days."

"Yes they have, Kwantie."

"What's that, Kim?"

"Now his white ass is on the floor taking the ass kicking and looking up to us black women, and begging for his life. Oh my! How times have changed, Kwantie!"

"Kwantie, is that you, baby? Help me! Something is wrong! I can't move my arms or legs. The last thing I remember was getting shot by some little dirty kid on the west side. And then some chick tried to kill me, so I ran her ass over trying to get the fuck from outta there," Cash said.

"You stupid bastard! I should'a known that was your dumb ass! I should'a known you had something to do with that!" Rooney responded.

"Rooney, is that you? What the fuck is going on here?"

"Hell if I know. I was waiting on Kane at the club,

and the next thing I know, I'm tied the fuck up in this car with your ass."

"Where the fuck is Kane at? Is my nigga okay?"

"I hope they haven't gotten to him yet, Cash. He's our only hope."

As Cash began to adjust his eyes, he started to realize that Kim was sitting right in front of him. He thought he was seeing double at first because Kwantie and Kim were dressed alike. Once his eyes had fully adjusted and he was able to see Kim's face, it didn't take him long to figure out that Kane was the one behind this, or the Mexicans had already taken him out and had bribed the two chicks into getting to him and Rooney. "Kwantie, what's going on, baby? Take these ropes off of me and let's get the fuck outta here before those Taco Bell eating amigos come back."

"Cash, I'm sorry, baby, but ain't no amigos coming back."

"Fuck you mean?"

"Baby, this is bigger than them. You must have forgotten that you wanted me dead. Remember, you had Nut take me to the country and he was supposed to kill me. But his stupid ass wanted to use me as an insurance policy just in case none of your plans panned out. Guess what? It didn't pan out. His bitch ass is dead. He's out there in the country, tied the fuck up to a chair full of bullet holes in his body, and with flies and maggots crawling all over him!"

"Kwantie, who the fuck did some shit like that to my man?"

"Me, bitch ass nigga! I killed him! I killed your man, just like I'm gonna kill your bitch ass! Cash, just tell me how could you not want all of this pussy? I was sexing you like crazy. I would have done anything in the world for you. But now I'm with Kane, and I'm the happiest bitch you could ever meet." Leaning over to whisper in his ear, she told him about her and Kim as well.

"Thanks to your gay ass, me and Kim are freaking each other and are enjoying every minute of it. And before the sun rises in the morning, we'll be fucking Kane, and that's because he's more of a man than your gay ass will ever be. To top that off, when we're done with him, the city will be ours. Me and Kim will be running shit."

"Who da fuck you calling gay?"

"You, you punk bitch! I left a camcorder recording in the house one day and it recorded you and Nut. When I came home and watched it, it disgusted me. It's bad enough that you were fucking a man in my house and letting him suck your dick on my couch, but at least you could've gotten one that looked like a female. But you had Nut, a 6′ 5″ black ass silver back gorilla with corn rows, sucking your dick. You make me so sick, you nasty muthafucka!"

Kim couldn't believe what she had just heard. She wondered why he would rape her if he liked men. Before she could snap out of her thoughts, Kwantie had jumped on top of Cash and was scratching and punching at him. At first, Kim was unable to pull her off, but from all of the anger she had built up in her, she joined in and started helping Kwantie release her tension.

Standing outside of the car, Country noticed that the Limo was moving and opened the door to see what was going on. At first he wanted to let the two women beat Cash to death, but Kane gave him the word to pull them off and out of the car.

Still in shock, Rooney looked up and saw Kane's face and started to smile, thinking that Kane was there to save him and Cash. He was delighted.

Once Country got the women out of the car and

they had straightened themselves up, José just smiled and introduced himself. Kane had already explained to him who they were and how they were able to handle themselves.

Liking what he saw, he turned back to the action taking place in the car. Country had pulled out one of those big ass Rambo knives, and Rooney's eyes had almost popped out of his head, thinking that Country was about to do him bodily harm. He was so scared that he didn't even realize that Country had reached in and cut the knots that bound his wrists and ankles. Rooney had closed his eyes and started yelling at the top of his lungs.

Cash looked up and started thanking Country once he saw him cut the knots on Rooney's ropes. Nervous himself, he was telling Country about the Mexicans that had set him up and how they had tried to kill him.

Country just stared at him in disbelief. Stepping back out of the car, he kept his eyes on Cash and Rooney.

Rooney was the first one to get out of the car, and when he did, he damn near froze in his tracks. *"El Diablo!"*

"Si, papi!"

Rooney thought that he was seeing a ghost. José standing next to Kane had almost given him a heart attack where he stood. Reaching for his chest and almost falling, Country caught him by his neck. His knees had become weak. He really didn't know what was going on, and at this point, he wasn't sure if he really wanted to know. If both men were standing there together, he knew that it could only mean one thing for him.

Stepping out the car behind him, Cash was talking shit without a care in the world. At first sight, seeing Kane and a Mexican standing together had made him smile. Remembering the plan, he knew that they had finally made it to the top of the game. Rooney was the bait. He was proud of his cousin, thinking what a mastermind he was. "Big cuz, what da fuck are we doing here at the storage? I thought we were gonna kill this piece of shit and get the fuck out of the States."

"Lil' cuz, all that is still gonna happen, but there's been a slight adjustment in the plans. See, before we go any further, I must ask you one question, and don't lie to me. What da fuck is on the other side of that gate?"

"Kane, cuz, what are you talking about? I kidnapped Carp's son for old Rooney here. I just kept him for a little insurance just in case we needed a ticket out of the game if Rooney or Carp ever came at us with some bullshit."

"So, Cash, you mean to tell me when Country opens that gate up, we'll see Carp's son on the other side of it, and nothing or nobody else? The only reason I'm asking is that José here is missing two of his brothers."

"Kane, that's my word."

Kane gave Country a nod, and knew that shit was about to hit the fan. "Country, hold up. Cash, you say Carp's son is in there, right? Well, who da fuck is driving my Limo?"

Shawn opened the door and stepped out of the Limo. Cash's face froze in shock while Country opened the gate at the same time.

José turned around and saw his two brothers tied up and badly beaten to an unrecognizable state. "*Papi*, what the fuck is this?"

"José, see, your two brothers and Cash paid two white cops to kill my little brother. My cousin, Cash here set the whole thing up. Rooney was the mastermind behind the whole thing. I didn't kill your brothers because I feel that you should handle it. In my family, when you don't follow orders, you die. There ain't no hard feelings, but when playing this game, everyone knows there ain't no rules.

You know just as well as I do that there's no honor among thieves. Business is business. Now, loyalty and your word do go a long way."

"*Papi*, you're right. Not just in your family, but in my country and in this business, when you don't follow instructions, you die as well. But at our level, we don't get our hands dirty no more. But because it is our family member, we have to."

"José, may I suggest something?" Kane and José whispered amongst each other for a few moments, walked back out of the storage bin towards Country, and then they both pulled out.

"El Diablo, wait! Let me explain! Kane, please hear me out. I'm the one that brought your ass into this. I raised you to be the man that you are now. I'm the one that introduced you to José. This is how you repay me? And José, I hooked you up with this nigga. If it wasn't for me neither one of you would be where you're at today."

"Shut da fuck up, cracker! I never liked your ass anyway. I should have killed your ass a long time ago."

"Fuck you, José!"

"Well, Rooney, our journey has come to an end tonight. I'll be sure to let Country keep fucking your secretary. And as far as your wife, well, she loves black meat! I've been fucking her since I was in high school. Right now you should be honored to die by me and José's hands."

Rooney fell to his knees, looked both of them in their eyes and swallowed. The first bullet knocked a chunk of his skull off, while Kane's 50 cal blew a hole so big in the side of his face that the blood squirted on Country's white T-shirt.

Turning around and walking back into the bin, José went and kissed his two brothers on the cheek, and explained to them in Spanish what was about to happen. Looking over his shoulder, he saw the two females walking towards him, each with a Glock in their hand. José nodded and stepped out of the way as they emptied their entire clips. Never looking back, he walked out of the bin.

As the girls walked out, Country grabbed Rooney's lifeless body and tossed it into the bin with the other two. The night was almost complete.

When Cash noticed that Country had slid behind him, he made up his mind that he wasn't going out like the rest of them. He had in his mind that somebody was dying with him tonight. Making a quick turn, he hit Country in the mouth, then again with two body shots. When Country toppled over, Cash grabbed his gun and started shooting.

Being that Country was the closest, he dove to the ground and took cover.

José grabbed Kim and Kwantie as the bullets started flying.

Kane didn't take cover. His instincts made him pull his gun out and start shooting back.

Cash got lucky and got two quick shots off, hitting Kane in the chest and knocking him down. Kwantie started screaming as Cash was walking up on him from the front of the Limo. As he passed the driver's door, he was walking up on Kane to finish the job as Kane lay stretched out at the back of the Limo. Standing over him, he reached down and turned his body over so that Kane could remember his face before he sent him to hell.

Looking up, Kane just watched as Cash pointed his gun at his face and continued to talk shit. While in mid-sentence, Cash's head exploded off of his shoulders, and his body fell right on top of his. Kane was just happy to see Shawn, the Limo driver for the night standing there with a smoking, sawed off double barrel shot gun.

Pulling up to Hangar Bay 5 at the old airport, Country was helping Kane walk. The two shots had knocked the wind out of him, but didn't penetrate his bulletproof vest.

As everyone boarded José's G-5 jet with their personal belongings, Kane walked over to Shawn and shook his hand.

José walked back down the steps of the private jet and handed Shawn a black Nike gym bag full of money for saving their lives, and gave him a manila envelope with his father's name on it. "Kane, are you ready, *papi*? Let's get the fuck out of here."

"A'ight, give me a second, José. Shawn, tell your father I said congratulations." No more words were spoken between them. Kane turned and limped away with the help of Country. Pausing as he reached the top of the steps, he turned and tossed the keys to the young man, and told him where to drop the Excursion off.

Leaving the Limo at the hangar bay, Shawn smiled, and knew that whatever Kane had left at the rental place was his for the keeping. As the doors closed, he saluted the plane and got the hell out of there.

Somewhere on a beach in Puerto Rico, Lexus and Steph were entertaining JB and E-Dubb in the water, while Country had two women from the club entertaining him as well.

José and Kane sat on the beach with two bottles of the most expensive imported wine they could afford, while working out further details of their partnership. They both had taken a major loss, but they knew at any given time in the game that if a man goes to jail or gets killed, there are always five to ten more young goons ready to replace them. And out of those, maybe two would really be worth something.

José tipped his glass towards Kane. Giovanni continued to rub Kane's shoulders and chest. José just smiled, looked up at his Puerto Rican chick and grabbed her hand and ran towards the water to join the rest of the crew.

Sitting inside a private shack enjoying each other, Kim and Kwantie were going at it so hard that they had lost track of the time that they had been away.

Walking up towards the private shack, Kane had plans to introduce Kwantie to Giovanni to see if the time was right for them to complete their discussion. When they reached the door, he turned the doorknob, and he and Giovanni proceeded to the back of the shack.

Reaching the back, Kane heard noises but wasn't sure where they were coming from. Slowly opening the door, he caught the girls in the act, and couldn't even get mad. He just started smiling as his dick got hard while he watched Kim's pretty little ass in the air while eating Kwantie out.

Not hearing the door open, they were busy enjoying themselves. Kwantie held her legs up in the air, pulling them further back to her head and opening her lips for Kim to suck on.

Clearing his throat to get their attention had startled them. Seeing Kane standing there with Giovanni made them stop and wonder what he was about to say.

"Damn, Kwantie! I was bringing Giovanni in here to complete our fantasy, and you're already at it with Kim. What, y'all couldn't tell me? What am I supposed to do now?"

Kim didn't hesitate. She looked up and got off the bed, and she and Kwantie walked over to the both of them and started kissing Giovanni. Grabbing her hand, they began to undress her and Kane.

Kwantie and Kim both looked up at Kane and said, "Baby, we love you and we both want you, and we both are willing to accept each other. We know what you do in the streets. We wanted to surprise you for your birthday, but you in turned surprised us. So, now that we're here, we all might as well enjoy ourselves. If Giovanni doesn't have a problem with us, we definitely don't have a problem with her joining us to please you. The more the merrier!"

Kane smiled and shut the door.

Chapter 24

Back in the States, Mitch and Thomas knew they had to do something a.s.a.p. Pulling up on the scene of the crime, they could already smell the burning flesh of the dead officers' bodies in the fire when they opened the doors to the truck.

"Mitch, do you believe this shit? This is crazy! Those bastards tried to take out the whole entire damn police task force!"

"Yeah, Thomas. But the worst thing about it is that they were trying to take us out too. They wanted us to be inside that damn club tonight. It if wasn't for that emergency call, our asses would be dead as well."

"Fuck that shit, Mitch! I'ma kill that muthafucking black ass nigger, Kane myself. As soon as we can catch his ass, he's mine!"

"Calm down, Thomas. We have a bigger fish to fry right now. I got a trick up my sleeve for Carp's black ass." Mitch's mind was running a hundred miles per hour. All he could think about was getting revenge for all of his fallen comrades.

Getting out of their unmarked police truck, all they could see was the other officers standing around crying. Seeing all of this mayhem, tears had filled their eyes instantly.

They knew this situation was getting out of control. They knew with Mayor Rooney dead, they would be on their own. Between the both of them, they had enough money to walk away, but their greed would not allow them to just quit. But when greed sets in and starts to question the mind, someone will answer the call.

As they made their way around, Mitch and Thomas were trying to take in every little detail they could. Everybody that was anybody was in attendance. Everyone from the governor to the news media had gathered at the remains of what used to be a club. Every news station and their helicopters were there trying to be the first ones to broadcast the live event.

"Good evening. This is Tonya Wilson from Channel Six News. I'm sorry for interrupting your scheduled broadcast, but there has been a disastrous event. It is too terrible and horrifying to show on television, but I can assure you that officers of the City of Anderson, South Carolina Police Department have been attacked."

"I am now being told that our own Mayor Rooney might have been attending this so called police bash. As of right now we're not sure of his whereabouts, and are still awaiting confirmation."

"Ladies and gentlemen, we here at Channel Six

News need your help. We have to stand up and join forces to regain control of our communities. These street hoodlums have gone too far this time. When does it stop? Everywhere you look, violence is taking over what used to be a beautiful place to live. Let me ask you, the viewers a question: Whatever happened to the days of not locking our doors? I'll tell you. They have been replaced by guns!"

"I apologize for my sudden outburst, but I'm just so tired of living in fear."

"I will keep you all posted on any updates. Please, if you have any information, please don't hesitate to contact 1-800-CRIME-STOPPERS…"

"Cindy, since my husband is gone for the night, let's sit down and have some me and you time. You know it's been a while since we sat and talked."

"Mrs. Rooney, you're right. It has been a long time since we just sat and talked. I'm going to fix us a drink. What will you have?"

"Fix me a cranberry and vodka."

While Cindy fixed their drinks, Mrs. Rooney went into the living room and turned on the big 67 inch flat screen television. Before she could get to the station she wanted, she saw that almost every channel had some kind of news reporter who was broadcasting live. At first she couldn't hear what was being said, so she turned on the surround sound and adjusted the volume.

By the time she got the volume adjusted, she wasn't sure if she had heard the news reporter right, so she turned to Channel Six just in the nick of time to catch Tonya Wilson reporting the situation about her husband. The last thing

Mrs. Rooney heard before passing out was:

> *"...Mayor Rooney was supposed to be attending this so called police bash, but we're not sure of his whereabouts at this time..."*

The loud noise from her dropping to the floor and the remote slipping out of her hand and shattering the expensive glass table startled Cindy. Without hesitation, Cindy put the bottle of vodka down and ran into the living room where she was shocked to find Mrs. Rooney on the floor going into convulsions.

Unaware of what had happened, Cindy picked up the cordless phone that was on the table next to where Mrs. Rooney had fallen and dialed 911. Screaming and yelling at the top of her lungs into the phone only made the situation worse. The operator on the other end of the phone put her on hold.

Cindy turned around and froze with terror when she saw what was on the television. When she saw Mayor Rooney's face included with the list of members of the force to be honored and remembered, she almost past out herself.

The 911 operator had come back on line when Cindy explained that it was the mayor's wife that needed the emergency assistance.

Carp had pulled up on the scene a few minutes after Mitch and Thomas did. Parking his black Lexus 400, Carp jumped out and went straight into detective mode. He had his note pad out and was jotting down any and all of the information that he could. Looking around, he tried to keep a close eye on Mitch and Thomas, but he had no worries because they were watching him just as closely.

After conversing with the C.S.I. team, Carp made his way around to talk with other departments to see what he could find out.

Taking notes from everyone and comparing them was going to take some studying of every word and detail. Carp knew that everyone had a long night ahead of him, and he was already tired. He had already made his mind up that he was leaving in the next 30 minutes.

Watching his every step, Carp was making his way back to his car as he looked around. He just shook his head as he looked at the scene. He knew Kane had something up his sleeve, but he would have never dreamed it was on this level. Finally reaching his car, he just stood there with a smirk before getting in.

"Thomas, get the truck and meet me on the corner."

As Mitch made his way through the rubbish, Thomas had ran and got the truck and parked around the corner and waited for Mitch.

Never looking up, Mitch kept his eyes locked on Carp's every move. By the time Carp got into his car and pulled off, Mitch was already sitting in the truck with Thomas waiting to follow Carp.

Pulling into the driveway, Shawn had just gotten home when his mother was rushing out of the door.

"Hey, Ma. Where are you going at this time of night in such a rush?"

"Hey, Shawn. Duty calls. The hospital called me back in. They said they need every hand available; something about a bomb going off at a club. Anyway, I left you a plate in the microwave just in case you're hungry. I love you, and I'll see you in the morning. Whose truck is that? Never mind, I don't even want to know!"

Shawn couldn't say a word. Kane had basically given him a brand new Range Rover. It had only been a few hours since Kane and his crew had boarded the private jet and flew away.

Shawn knew that there was no time difference between South Carolina and Puerto Rico, and the only time it was different was in the winter when the clocks in the U.S. changed by one hour. He was wondering about what they were doing right now. Other than that, he knew that they were somewhere chilling and enjoying themselves. He was not upset at all. He walked away with a brand new Range Rover and more money than he could possibly count.

Watching his mother pull out of the driveway, he just stood there smiling, because he knew what he had just gotten away with.

Once his mother's car was out of sight, he grabbed the black gym bag and the yellow envelope that José had given him to give to his father, and went into the house.

Making his way up the stairs, he dropped the black gym bag on the floor at his bedroom door, went down the hallway to his parents' room and tossed the yellow envelope on the bed. He knew his father would be home before his mother, so his father would see the envelope first.

Driving without a care in the world, Carp did not notice the black SUV following him. He was trying to read some of the notes that he had taken down while at the explosion. His body was weakened with exhaustion, and he was becoming sleepy.

He had just turned onto his street and still had not looked in his rearview mirror. Reaching his driveway, he was so tired that he almost passed his own home due to not seeing his wife's car in the driveway. Instead, he saw a Range Rover in his driveway.

Turning into the driveway, Carp couldn't believe his eyes. One part of him was happy to know that Shawn was home and had made it safely and in one piece. But looking at a brand new black Range Rover in his driveway could bring trouble.

As he sat in the car anticipating his next move, he noticed headlights turning onto his street, but realized they stopped a few houses down so he quickly blew it off, not caring.

Down the street, Mitch and Thomas had just pulled up and turned their truck lights off. Sitting there for a few minutes, they were becoming agitated.

Finally after fifteen minutes, Carp got out of the car and walked around the new truck parked in his driveway, admiring its beauty. After walking twice around the truck, he pulled out his keys and made his way into the house. Before closing the door, he looked up and down the street just to check to see if anything was out of the ordinary.

Being so tired, Carp walked straight into the house and shut the front door, setting the alarm. He took his sweet time walking up the stairs as he quickly scanned the living room.

Once he reached the top of the stairs, Carp made his way down the hallway toward his bedroom. As he approached Shawn's room, he tapped on the door and waited for a response before just barging in. Not getting an answer, he tapped a couple of more times. He was trying to respect his son's privacy at first, but got fed up and just opened the door and peeked in, hoping that his son wasn't doing anything crazy. When he opened door wide enough to see what was going on, he was surprised to find Shawn lying in the bed with his headphones on and music blasting in his ears.

Carp just giggled to himself, and knew why Shawn never answered his door. Closing the door, he turned and proceeded to his bedroom.

"One-two-three… one-two-three… one-two-three! Breathe! Breathe, Mrs. Rooney! Don't you quit on me! Hold on, we're almost there!"

The ambulance driver was driving as fast as he could. Cindy was in the back with the other paramedic, watching as he gave Mrs. Rooney C.P.R. and tried to revive her.

Mrs. Rooney's vitals were not good. Just looking at her, everyone thought she was in the best of health, but seeing her husband's face on the television screen had given her a heart attack or a stroke. Because of who she was, the best doctors were awaiting her arrival at the hospital's emergency room. When the ambulance finally pulled up, her vitals were still down. The team of doctors had her out of the ambulance and into Anderson Memorial in record time. They were determined to save her life. Once in the E.R. they went to work.

She had no pulse and had flat lined. Not giving up, the doctors kept fighting. They shocked her heart with the defibrillator, and the heart monitor came to life with a beeping sound. Mrs. Rooney's life had been saved.

Chapter 25

Mitch and Thomas sat in the truck and carefully watched every little detail. Thomas was eager to just get out of the truck and kill Carp, but Mitch had other plans.

Noticing the new truck in the driveway, Mitch knew his plan was foolproof. "Hey Thomas, would you get a load of this shit! Mr. Uppity Negro has a fucking Range Rover parked in his driveway. Now, you mean to tell me he can afford a truck like this and a Lexus 400 on his got-damn salary? Mr. Don't Do Nothing, Mr. Straight Guy, Mr. I Follow All the Rules? Well, it looks like he's no different than we are."

"Mitch, who would've ever thought that Carp was crooked, or even on someone's payroll?"

"Not me, Thomas. Not in a million years. But if he has this new truck in his driveway, then he has to have some dead presidents stashed somewhere in that damn house, and we need that, partner."

While looking through the binoculars, Thomas

noticed the upstairs bedroom light come on. That was the sign that they were waiting on. Grabbing their bulletproof vests and checking their guns, Mitch tossed Thomas a pair of surgical Latex gloves just to make sure they didn't leave any fingerprints behind. Time was of the essence, and they knew they could not afford to make any mistakes. Once they were ready, Mitch told Thomas to slowly let the truck roll down the street and park in front of Carp's driveway.

Within minutes, Mitch and Thomas were parked in front of the house and out of the car, and were walking across the grass.

While creeping across the well manicured grass, Mitch noticed the security system sign posted in the yard. He knew with the type of vehicles Carp had in the driveway and the quality of the neighborhood, that the security system sign was not a fake. "Hey Thomas, we have a problem. The uppity Negro has an alarm system hooked up to his house."

"Come on, Mitch. That's easy to bypass. I used to read up on those damn things all the time. All we need is a piece of foil, and bam!"

"Where the hell are we gonna find some got-damn foil at a time like this?" Mitch watched as his partner pulled his wallet out and fiddled around until he came up with what they were looking for. "Thomas, what the hell… never mind, I'm not even gonna ask." Thomas had pulled a small piece of foil out of his wallet to make use of it. Once they got to the front door, Mitch watched as Thomas went to work on the alarm system.

The lock didn't stand a chance against Thomas. He had picked the lock and slid the piece of foil in between the two metal magnets that would cause the alarm system to go off.

Entering his bedroom, Carp was so tired that he didn't even notice the yellow envelope lying on the bed. He had the same routine every night when he came in from work. The first thing he always did was take his gun out of its holster and lay it on the nightstand, and then go into the bathroom and stare into the mirror and thank God for giving him another day.

After that, he turned and walked out of the bathroom, but he stopped in his tracks once he finally saw the yellow envelope on the bed. It took him by surprise at first, because he usually didn't miss something that noticeable. He hesitated for a second until he saw his name on it.

Opening the envelope, Carp sat on the edge of the bed quickly once looking at the contents of the package. Shocked to death, he almost lost his breath. He had to reach over to his nightstand and pour himself a glass of cognac straight, no ice no chaser. He couldn't believe his eyes.

José had opened an offshore account in his name. Plus, he included some pictures of the two men who had been responsible for his father's death. Attached to the pictures were two notes that he read:

> *Mr. Carpenter, you don't know me or anything about me, but your son does. He's a good kid who's caught up in this street life shit. I'm only giving you this information as a favor to Kane. What you didn't know was that your father and Kane's father were cool back in New York, so thank Kane.*
>
> *Mr. Carpenter, the guy they call "Reverend" is locked up in a penitentiary located in Coleman, Florida.*

The other man is known as "Mr. Untouchable", Mickey Banks. Just to let you know, Mickey is somewhere in the federal witness protection program. I'm sorry for what happened to your father, but that's part of the game we play.

The other information, well, let's just say I know you're trying to move up in the ranks. Here are two of your very own. These two crooked ass cops are no good. Here is some paperwork you can use to put their asses away if you choose to use it. These are two very dangerous men. Hopefully they have attended the police bash and have already been taken care of, but if not, hopefully you can use this information.

Mr. Carpenter, this is not bribery money or turn the other cheek money. This is going ahead and retire and get the fuck out of the way money. This shit is bigger than you, trust me!

"Excuse me, ma'am. What is your name and relationship to the mayor's wife?"

"First of all, her name is Mrs. Rooney. My name is Miss Cindy Palico, and I'm no relation to her, I've been assigned to her. I'm her personal secretary. Do you have a problem with that?"

"No, ma'am. I didn't mean a thing by it. Would you sign here on the dotted line so I can start processing her paperwork?"

"I apologize. It's been a long day and I'm just worried about Mrs. Rooney's wellbeing right now. Do you know how she's doing?"

"Well, not at the present time, but give me a few moments and I'll go to E.R. and check on her."

"Thank you."

Standing in the living room, Mitch and Thomas had their guns out, ready for any drama. Before making their way up the stairs, they stood there quietly scanning the living room until their eyes had become adjusted to the darkness. It didn't take long.

Creeping up the stairway, Mitch went first as Thomas brought up the rear. They had broken the law so many times that it had become natural to them. There was no need for talking. They had a mutual understanding between the both of them.

Once they made it to the top of the stairs, Mitch noticed that there were four doors in the hallway. Pointing his gun at the first two, Thomas knew he meant for him to check them out.

Twisting the doorknob, Thomas opened it slowly and peeked his head in, only to find that it was empty. Moving on to the next room, he repeated the same movements, but this time he had a different outcome when he stuck his head in the bedroom door. He looked back at Mitch and gave him the signal that someone was in the room.

Creeping down the dimly-lit hallway, Mitch peeked his head into the room to find Shawn lying in the bed with his head phones on as loud as they possibly could be. At first Mitch was going to shoot him, but then had second thoughts because Carp might hear the gunshot and come running to the rescue. Mitch looked back at Thomas and closed the door as quietly as he possibly could.

Making their way further down the hallway, the next room that they came upon was a bathroom. Looking around before moving on, nothing seemed to be out of the ordinary.

Looking at each other, they knew that the next room would be the one they were looking for. Carp would be in there. This was what they had come for. Ready or not, they knew that there was no turning back. These were the moments they hated. They knew that this could go two ways, but they were hoping for the easy way tonight.

As they got to the last door, Mitch noticed that the door wasn't all of the way closed. Putting his ear to the door first, he was trying to take all of the necessary precautions to come out of this situation alive. No guts, no glory was the motto that he and Thomas went by.

After reading the letter, Carp got up and poured himself another drink. This was what he fought against every day. The evil doings, the corruption, the drug dealing, all of the negativity in the world, and now he was being faced with it himself.

This was one of those choices that would require some thinking. He knew that if he called the number that José had given him, he would be no different from the scum he fought against every day.

To him, it wasn't about the money; it was about the oath he took: Justice, freedom, and making it safe in the streets for everyone. But he knew in his heart that if he took the money from José and Kane, everything he had done up to this point would be worthless.

Standing in the doorway of the bathroom, he stared in the mirror as he swallowed the last of the cognac in his glass. Setting his glass on the edge of the sink, he turned the water on to fill up the tub.

While the water was running, he pulled the pictures

out of the yellow envelope and looked at them again. Staring at the two men who had killed his father started his mind racing. He knew he could never get into the prison system to catch up with the man they called Reverend, but he knew if he could get accepted into the Federal Bureau of Investigation, he had a good chance of tracking down Mickey Banks.

After staring at the pictures, Carp slid them back in the yellow envelope and took one more look at the check and all of the zeros on it. Tempted by greed, he shook his head and set the envelope on the sink next to his empty glass.

The steam from the hot water was filling up the bathroom to the point where Carp could barely see. Standing up to take his clothes off, he thought he heard a noise but wasn't sure. At first he thought it was the alcohol, but he heard another squeaking noise and was sure that he wasn't hearing things.

Walking out of the bathroom, he was pulling his T-shirt over his head as he went to check things out.

"Miss Palico! Paging Miss Palico Please report to the front desk!"

As Cindy reached the front desk, the nurse had a friendly smile on her face as she explained to her what was going on.

"Miss Palico, I'm glad to inform you that Mrs. Rooney will be all right. We're still not sure, but we think that she suffered a slight heart attack or a mild stroke. Can you tell me what she was doing right before she passed out?"

"Yes. We were about to sit and relax and engage in a little girl talk, and the last thing I remember was the television coming on. She must have seen her husband's face all over the news."

"Thank you, Miss Palico. I have to go report this to the doctors in the E.R. I'm pretty sure that it's nothing. Please don't go anywhere. I've listed you as her next of kin. Right now the doctors are running more tests on her to make sure she's stable."

"Thank you, and I apologize for being so rude when I first came in. I appreciate everything you have done for me, and especially for Mrs. Rooney."

"Don't worry, Miss Palico. I'm used to that."

Chapter 26

"Ladies and gentlemen, I know it's late—or should I say early in the morning. Everyone here has a part to play. J-B and E-Dubb, y'all handled your business very well. Kwantie and Kim, I couldn't have done better myself. Big Country, if it wasn't for you homie, I don't know where I'd be right now. You always pop up at the right time."

"It's sad to say, but even though we lost a few good people, we're here and we will stay on top. First off, we lost my brother, Jason. I'll miss him no matter what. Cash and Nut, even though they were in their own world, I'll forever respect their gangsta. If it wasn't for them, the streets wouldn't respect us the way that they do."

"I have to give thanks to Mayor Rooney, even though he was a piece a shit. He's the one that basically taught me and Big Country everything we know about this game and the streets. When I tell you that we will win some and lose some, there's one thing I can promise you for sure: We will win more than we lose."

"I have one more thank you He's not here physically, but his spirit is with us every time we move. To the man who saved my life tonight. I want to say thank you, Shawn, wherever you are right now."

"So please, everybody put your glasses in the air and let's have a moment of silence for the fallen and the forgotten soldiers, and let's have a moment of silence for us, the ones who made it. I told y'all that the grass was much greener on the other side. Just trust me when I say it can only get better."

"Excuse me, Mr. Woodson. *Senor* José needs to see you. He said it's an emergency."

Hearing the water running in the bathroom gave Mitch and Thomas just enough time to slide into the bedroom without being heard.

Looking around, Thomas noticed Carp's service revolver on the nightstand next to the bed. Tiptoeing over to pick it up, the floorboards started squeaking. Trying to be as quiet as he could, he knew he had to move swiftly before Carp came out to check on the noise.

"Vanessa, is that you, baby?"

Hearing Carp's voice, Mitch hurried across the bedroom and posted up beside the bathroom door. He knew that he and Thomas had only a few seconds before Carp would come out to check on the noise. And just as they thought, Carp's shadow approached the doorway.

Stepping through the doorway, Carp was unaware of the danger that was about to happen to him. He had just pulled his T-shirt over his head when he thought he saw a shadowy figure in the corner of his eye. The look on his face when he saw Thomas standing there in the middle of his bedroom startled him to the point of fear. After just seeing his face in the photos that José and Kane had sent to him, he knew that Mitch was not too far away. His mind instantly went to defense mode, and he worried about what could happen next if he didn't play his cards right. But before he could get a word out of his mouth, Mitch hit him in the back of his head with the butt of his gun, knocking him down instantly.

"Thomas, grab his feet. We need to get him down the hallway before the kid in the other room hears the commotion and comes to check it out."

Carp was only semiconscious. As soon as Thomas grabbed his feet, he began twisting and kicking, trying to get loose from their grasp.

Mitch had lost his grip and fell to the floor. Trying to wrestle with Carp was the wrong thing to do. Carp had overpowered him easily.

Still dazed, Carp had gotten loose from Thomas's grip, but he lost his balance and fell against the bed. This jostled the phone, which dropped to the floor and under the bed.

Jumping on his back, Mitch wrapped his arms around Carp's neck and started squeezing until his lock was getting tighter and tighter, cutting his airway off. This caused Carp to drop down to one knee, and then all the way down to the floor until he was finally unconscious.

"Mitch, let him go! You're gonna kill his ass! He's out cold already. Let him go. He ain't gonna be any good to us if he's dead."

Loosening his grip, Mitch let go of the hold around Carp's neck. As he got up off the bedroom floor, Thomas lifted Carp's body up and tossed him over his shoulder like a bag of potatoes and carried him out of the room.

Trying to be as quiet as he could, Thomas was

creeping down the hallway, hoping to make it past Shawn's bedroom before Carp woke up again and started making noise.

Looking around the room, Mitch turned to walk out, hoping that they didn't leave any evidence behind that could link them to this kidnapping.

Making it to the stairs, Thomas managed to carry Carp all the way down without any problems.

As Mitch came down the stairs, he was so focused on what he was going to do to Carp that he had forgotten about the foil that was between the two magnets that was preventing the alarm from sounding.

Thomas had already gone out the door without tripping the alarm and was putting Carp into the trunk, when Mitch went through the door, causing the alarm to go off.

After following the lady to the private room, she stepped aside and pointed, indicating for Kane to enter through the double wooden doors.

Kane didn't know what to expect on the other side of the doors, but he knew he had no choice but to go through them and find out. Kane knew that José was a major figure. When he stepped in and the door had shut behind him, he had no idea what was waiting for him.

"*Hola, papi!* It's been a while."

Seeing Isabella standing there naked had made him smile. Looking around the room, Kane had become very skeptical. "*Hola, Senorita*. It has been a while."

"Come, *papi*. I want you right now!"

"Isabella, isn't your uncle right next door? We can't do it while he's here. You know how you like to scream, baby."

"Why not? These walls are very thick. He won't hear us, I promise." Isabella had made her mind up that she was going to have Kane inside of her tonight, no matter what it took. Ever since he had arrived at the mansion, she was determined to get him in her room. "*Papi,* I want you. Please! Just put it in me. I want to feel you inside my stomach."

The more she talked, the closer she was getting to Kane. And before he knew it, she was in his arms and kissing him. Rubbing her body, Kane knew he had to hurry up before José returned to the party.

While they were kissing, she was already rubbing and stroking his dick. She now had his full attention. As soon as she felt his dick growing in her hands, she dropped down on her knees and pulled his dick out of his white linen shorts and began sucking and kissing the tip of it, while slobbering and bobbing her head up and down.

Standing there watching her, Kane enjoyed every stroke. He grabbed her by the chin and lifted her head up until she was face to face with him. "*Mami,* you sure you want me?"

"Yes, *papi*. Fuck me. I'm yours."

With nothing else needing to be said, Kane knew he was in a race against time. He picked Isabella up and carried her over to her bed and laid her down ever so gently. Any other time, he would have taken the time out to return the favor of oral sex, but that's not what she wanted right now. She wanted to feel Kane inside of her; she wanted to get fucked, and that's what Kane was about to do to her.

Spreading her legs apart, Kane stepped in between them and placed all ten inches of his manhood inside of her. Her legs started trembling and she was biting her bottom lip as he began to push in and out of her. She started moaning and squeezing her breasts as he began to pick up the pace.

Isabella started grinding her hips back and forth. She was humping Kane back with every deep thrust that he gave her. She threw it right back at him.

Looking down as he watched himself go in and out of her, he noticed the white, milky cream gushing out on his dick every time he would pull out of her. Knowing that she was cumming, he pulled all the way out and turned her over on her stomach. With her juices still flowing, he pushed himself right back into her, and with the quickness, she had his rhythm and was thrusting her hips right back at him, trying to take it all.

The moans had turned into grunts as Kane had her on all fours and was pounding and pumping as hard and deep as he could into her.

"*Si, papi! Si, papi!* Fuck me, *papi!* Beat my ass! I've been bad! Spank me, *papi!* Spank me! This is your po-nanny!"

Kane was so turned on that he started pulling Isabella's ponytail as he started slapping her on the ass. The harder he pushed inside of her and slapped her ass cheeks, the louder her moans got until she just buried her face into the pillow and started screaming at the top of her lungs.

"*Si, papi!* I'm cumming! Don't stop, *papi! Si... si,* that's it! I feel you inside my stomach. Cum... cum now!"

"I am, Isabella! I'm cummin', baby! I'm cummin'!"

Before he could finish saying that he was cumming, she slid off of his dick, turned around and put his dick between her breasts and squeezed them together with her mouth open until he finally shot off in her mouth, all over her face, and all over her breasts.

Looking down at Isabella as she held her tongue out,

Kane was excited when she grabbed his dick and started beating it against her tongue until he had finished.

Licking her lips and swallowing the rest of his jizz made Isabella a "must keep" on Kane's list of freaks.

"Thank you, *papi*. You can go now."

Pulling up his pants, Kane just turned and walked toward the door, trying to rush back to the party before José returned.

The alarm in the house went off, and it was so loud that it had startled Shawn. He jumped up and grabbed the gun that Kane had given him from under his mattress. Running to his bedroom door, he peeked out quickly, hoping that no one was stupid enough still to be in the house. Seeing no movement, he ran down the stairs, aiming his gun and ready to shoot anyone on sight. Halfway down the stairs, he noticed that the front door to the house was wide open.

He really became nervous and was so startled by the phone ringing that swung his arm around to shoot in the direction of the phone. But he stopped himself just in time and answered it instead. "Hello!"

"Hello, this is Keep Safe Security, and we noticed your alarm is going off. We are just calling to make sure everything is okay. Do you need us to send a police car to your residence?"

"No, ma'am. My father is a cop himself. Everything is okay. We were just moving some new furniture in and forgot that the alarm was set. I apologize."

"Well, before you hang up, please give me the four digit access code and your name so that I can verify that you're part of the residence."

"My name is Shawn Carpenter, and the four digit

code is 1-0-2-8."

"Thank you, Sir. Have a good evening."

As soon as the phone hung up, the alarm shut off on its own.

Shawn walked to the door and peered out to see if everything was clear. At first he didn't see anything and was about to shut the door, but he noticed his father's car parked right next to his truck. Stepping outside, he called for his father.

Yelling at the top of his lungs, he turned and ran back inside, slamming the door behind him. He ran up the stairs two steps at a time towards his parents' room. "Pops, where you at? You a'ight, Pops? Where are you?"

Reaching the bedroom, he noticed the door was cracked open. Pushing it open with the barrel of his gun, he was ready for whatever or whoever was on the other side of the door. "Pops, you in here? You a'ight? Say something! I'm coming in. It's me, Shawn. You a'ight?"

Looking around the room, he quickly noticed the bed was messed up a little and the lamp was lying on the floor. Seeing his father's gun on the floor was enough to alert him to some foul play.

Looking in the bathroom, he saw the empty glass on the edge of the sink and the yellow envelope that he specifically remembered leaving on the bed. Shawn couldn't figure out what was going on.

Going back into the bedroom, he bent down to pick up the lamp and the gun. Not paying attention, when he reached for the gun, he also grabbed something else from under the edge of the bed. It was a cell phone. One thing for sure, he knew it wasn't his parents' phone. The phone was just a little too expensive for their tastes.

Staring at the phone, he began going through the memory to see what he could find. Finally, he just hit redial, and when someone answered, he asked, "Hello, who's dis?"

"Who the fuck is this, and how did you get my number?"

"First of all, you stupid muthafuckers left your phone in my father's bedroom. Now, tell me, where the fuck is my pops? What kind of sick ass games are you bitches playing?"

"Listen, kid. You need to find Kane and get that phone to him. If he doesn't answer the next time I call, we are going to kill your fucking father. When you get in contact with him, give him the phone, and give him this message too: Tell him he missed, and now we're coming for his black ass. The hunted has now become the hunter!" Mitch hung up the phone.

Running to his room, Shawn had to find the emergency number that Kane had given him just in case he couldn't get in touch with him. "Hello, may I speak to José?"

"This is he."

Chapter 27

As everyone was partying, no one had noticed Kane's absence. To them, they were on top of the world right now. No one had a care in the world. They had just managed to kill most of the crooked cops on the Anderson Police Department Task force, and get out of the country undetected.

Stepping back into the room, Kane stood there for a few moments, looking at his crew as they celebrated their victory.

Kim and Kwantie had Giovanni sandwiched between them as they danced and grinded on each other to the sounds of the salsa music playing.

E-Dubb and JB were sitting back enjoying the women that they brought from the strip club, while Big Country was enjoying a few of the Puerto Rican hostesses that José had catering their little extravaganza.

"What's up, big homie? You just gonna stand there all night and look crazy, or are you gonna enjoy yourself, my nigga?"

"Big Country, I'm cool, homie. Y'all enjoy yourselves. The night is still young. Has José come back in yet?"

"Nah. Ain't no telling where he's at. As long as these beautiful women keep coming, I'm okay. This is paradise, cuz. I could live like this forever on the real, my nigga."

"Don't worry, Big Country. Our turn is coming. Trust me, cuz. That bitch is right around the corner. I promise you that."

After pulling up to the abandoned house out in the country, Mitch jumped out of the car to remove the padlock off of the chain, so his partner could pull up into the garage.

Out of sight, out of mind was what Mitch always told Thomas when they were out doing wrong. He knew that if no one could ever pinpoint their every move, then there was nothing to worry about.

Once the truck was in the garage, Mitch dragged Carp's lifeless body out of the back seat as Thomas grabbed his feet to help him carry Carp into the house.

As they carried Carp down the stairs, the temperature had changed dramatically. Mitch could see Thomas's breath coming out of his mouth and nose as he breathed hard.

Looking around the basement, Mitch knew that this was the perfect hideaway. There were no windows, no other doors, and no other means of escape other than through the one and only door that they just came through, and the lock was on the outside so Carp was fucked.

While Mitch stayed downstairs with Carp, Thomas ran back upstairs to grab the black gym bag that contained all of the equipment needed for them to handle their business. "Hey, Mitch, how do you want me to handle this?"

"Shit, take the duct tape and wrap it around his legs and wrists first. Then tape them to the arms and legs of the chair. Then wrap his whole body to the chair. I don't want him to be able to move anything but his lips and eyes."

"What do you want me to do with this rope?"

"Hell, tie his ass up with it too. I ain't playing, Thomas. I'm not letting this big payday get away from us this time."

"I feel you, partner. This is a big one if everything goes right. Tell me, Mitch; after all of these years we'll finally be able to handle our business and retire. What are you going to do?"

"I don't know about you, but I'm getting my family and getting the fuck out of South Carolina."

"You're damn right! We'd be fools to stick around here after we pull this caper off."

After they finished wrapping the tape and tying rope around Carp, they went back upstairs and decided on who was going to watch him first.

Thomas took the first day, and Mitch left to see what was going on in the streets. But before he left, he said, "Thomas, don't fuck with that nigger. He's a sneaky muthafucker. Don't talk to him—don't even go down there to check on his ass. If he has to shit or piss, oh well! He'll have to shit and piss on his got-damn self. Don't worry about feeding his ass. He'll be a'ight for a day or two. I'm pretty sure by the next phone call, when I give them the information and the instructions, they'll be ready to get this over with."

"A'ight, Mitch, I got it. You act like I'm going to go down there and untie his ass and just let him get up and walk the fuck up out of here. Are you crazy? Letting him go should be the least of your worries. Me killing his black ass should be your main concern."

"Thomas, just leave his ass where he is and don't go fucking with him."

Later that evening while everyone was enjoying themselves, José stepped out of the room to receive an emergency phone call.

"Hello, is this José?"

"Si, amigo. Quien es?"

"This is Shawn, the Limo driver from earlier tonight... Detective Carpenter's son."

"Hola, papi! What are you calling this number for?"

"Sir, you gave me your card and told me to use it if I ever had an emergency and couldn't get in contact with Kane. Right now, Kane isn't answering his phone, so I decided to call you."

"Well, what is the emergency?"

"Mr. José, is it okay to talk on this phone?"

"*Si*. Don't worry, it's scrambled."

"Well, after I left y'all at the airport earlier tonight, I did exactly like you and Kane told me to do. I dropped the Limo off and got the Range Rover. Then I went straight home to give my pops the yellow envelope, but he had not gotten home yet so I left it on his bed."

"Shawn, please don't tell me something has happened to the damn envelope!"

"No, Sir, but after that I went to my room and was listening to music with my headphones on. I had fallen asleep but was awakened by the alarm going off in the house. The next thing I know, the phone was ringing and the security company was asking me questions. When I went down to check the keypad, the front door to the house was wide open. I started calling for my pops but he never answered. That's when I ran back upstairs to his bedroom, and he wasn't there. I noticed that the yellow envelope wasn't on the bed and the bed was messed up. The lamp and his gun were on the floor beside the bed. But the most important thing is, I found a cell phone and hit redial, and the bastard who answered started talking shit."

"What did he say?"

"It was a male's voice. He said to tell Kane that he missed, and now they were coming for him. That's when the phone went dead."

"Oh yeah? Well don't worry about a thing. Kane will be back in the morning. We will get your father back. You have my word on that."

"Excuse me, everyone. I know y'all are having a great time. I don't mean to disturb you. Make yourselves at home. *Mi casa es su casa.* But right now I have to talk with Kane alone, so please excuse us."

Kane didn't like the look on José's face at first. He had that feeling in his stomach, as if he had been caught with his hand in the cookie jar.

"Kane, we have a big problem back in the States. Shawn just called me and explained to me that his father has been kidnapped."

"Kidnapped? By who?"

"The only message they left was that 'you missed, and now they're coming for you'."

"Coming for me, huh? They got a long way to come

and get me."

"*Papi*, I gave Shawn my word that we would get his father back."

"What are you saying, José?"

"I'm saying I need y'all to go back to the States and handle this. Kane, there's no way we can go ahead with our business ventures and have a problem that we know nothing about."

"I can respect that. Well, let me go tell the rest of the crew so they can get some rest." Kane couldn't believe his ears as he walked out of the room and headed down the hallway. Shaking his head in disbelief, he was trying to figure out who had enough guts to even think about coming at him like that.

Kidnapping Carp was something his crew would have done, but to send a message saying that he had missed had him puzzled. At first, he was hoping that it was all a game, but he didn't think José would ever play games of this nature.

Then he thought about Carp trying to play both sides of the law, and trying to lure him and his crew back to the States so that he could bust them.

As he continued walking along the long corridor, Kane had realized that Shawn was the one that made the call, so it had to be for real. He was hoping that this was serious and not a game, but he felt in his heart that Shawn wouldn't be playing any games like this.

Upon entering the room where his crew was partying, Big Country and Kwantie noticed the look on his face.

"Baby, you a'ight? Everything okay?" she asked.

"Kwantie, tell the DJ to kill the music, and tell everyone who ain't part of the crew to get the fuck out."

As Kwantie did as he ordered, the room became silent.

"Listen up, everyone. We have a problem back home."

"What's up, Kane?"

"Well, Shawn's father has been kidnapped. José just got the call. The message they left was that 'we missed, and now they're coming for us'. All I can say is that it has to be the cops, because ain't no other crew got enough balls to even try no shit like that. So listen up. The party is over for now. I need y'all to put y'alls' game faces back on for one more run. José will have the jet ready to go in the morning. We only have a few hours to get some rest, so make the best of it so we can hurry up and get back here to this place called paradise."

"Don't forget, Shawn is one of us, so we have to give him the same love that we would give one another if it was one of us in this predicament, and that's a 110%. Plus, José gave him his word that we would get his father back. So, if there's nothing else, I guess I'll be seeing y'all in the morning. Get some rest."

Chapter 28

"Good morning, Mrs. Rooney. I'm glad to see you're awake. How are you feeling?"

"Cindy, what happened?"

"Mrs. Rooney, you know I love you and wish the best for you. You know I'd never try to hurt you, right?"

"Cindy, what's wrong? You're starting to scare me."

"Mrs. Rooney, it's your husband. He was in a terrible accident last night. The police bash he attended; somehow the building exploded and went up in flames. The news reported no survivors."

"Oh my God! You're saying my husband was killed?"

"They haven't identified his body as of yet."

"Okay, but that still doesn't explain what I'm doing in the hospital."

"Well, last night we were about to sit and have some girl talk, and I guess when you turned on the television you saw the news broadcasting the situation and passed out. The doctors just wanted to run a couple of tests on you to determine whether you had a slight heart attack or a mild stroke."

"Well, tell me, Cindy. Which one was it? What are the results?"

"Calm down. The tests haven't come back yet, but it seems like you're okay. I guess all the exercising you do has paid off, huh?"

"Yeah, I guess. If you call having sex with Kane exercise, then it paid off. You need to get some exercise in your life!"

Don't worry, I'm going to just as soon as the time is right! Cindy thought to herself.

The first night had gone by, and Thomas was in the empty house doing nothing but watching old reruns and listening to Carp moaning. Thomas wanted to just grab his gun, go downstairs in the basement and use Carp for target practice. But as bad as he wanted to, he didn't. The only thing that was stopping him was the bigger picture. Mitch knew what he was doing, and they were about to get enough money to walk away.

All of the dope boys throughout the city and county knew Thomas and Mitch. If you were a major player in the game and were getting a lot of money, moving a lot of dope, or even had access to a lot of guns, you could buy your freedom from prison if you ever got caught by them. Thomas and Mitch were the type to pull you over and ask you what you had, and if you had anything of value, they wanted half with no questions asked.

Extorting hustlers was nothing new to Thomas and Mitch, but going at Kane was their biggest fish yet.

Snapping out of his thoughts when he heard Carp

squirming around made Thomas want to get up and go down stairs and punish him. It had been quite a few hours since Thomas had talked to Mitch, and he knew that Mitch would stop by after he had made his rounds.

The last thing Mitch had told Thomas was that he was going to stop by the department to find out what was going on. He wanted to know what the rest of the force knew, what they were doing, and what rumors and leads they were following, so that he could stay one step ahead of them.

"Good morning, ladies and gentlemen. Last night we had the worst attack on our police force, or on any police force in history. We lost more than twenty agents last night. I am appalled at this. Whoever did this must be brought up on charges and dealt with in a court of the law… but only after we have our time with them first!"

"I want every got-damn snitch and rat talking. Any person that looks like they know something better tell it. I want all of the confidential informants informing us."

"Y'all let those scumbags out there in the streets selling drugs know that there will be no money made until whoever did this is brought to justice. I mean, crack down on the crack heads, the junkies, the smokers, the pill poppers, the meth heads… everyone! The crack dealers make no money, the weed man makes no money… even the white boys and the Mexicans make no money."

"I want patrol cars at every entrance to every apartment complex. I want patrol cars and road blocks set up all over town. I want patrol cars parked outside of every bar, every club and every after hours spot. I don't want anyone making money. I want every illegal liquor and gambling spot shut down."

"Before I close, has anybody seen or heard from Carp? Nobody has heard anything, huh? Well, I would like to introduce y'all to one of the newest members on this case."

"Thank you, Captain. Ladies and gentlemen, until last night this was an in-house case, but because of the explosion, the number of officers killed and the fact that this was a planned attack, the F.B.I. has gotten involved."

"My name is not important as of right now. I have been working this case for some time. I'm still undercover as of right now, so I can't give you my name."

"I know the in's and out's of this crew like the back of my hand. If our guesses are correct, we are after the same person and the same crew, but the only difference is that we want their supplier. That person is Mr. Kane Woodson. We have been investigating this crew for quite a while. We are very close to closing this case."

"I also have a partner who's still undercover, and who relays everything that's going on to me. Everything your captain has told you to do, do it, and we will flush out the enemy with the quickness."

"I want you to sit back and think for a minute: What if it was one of you that got caught in that explosion? How would you want us to handle the case?"

"If there is any information regarding this case, please get it to one of my agents so we can look into it. This is *your* town and we're not here to step on any toes. We're here to assist you where it's needed. Thank you. Now, let's catch those bad guys!"

As the F.B.I. agent finished her statement, she noticed that one of the male officers had a funny look on his face. She stared him directly in his eyes as she was talking, not once ever breaking eye contact with him. She made a mental note to find out who he was and what he was about. But for right now, she didn't like the vibe she was getting from him.

Back in Puerto Rico, everyone was bright eyed and bushy tailed. Putting in work was what they lived for. Even though they were a little upset for having to cut their vacation short, they were just as eager to get back to the States so they could handle whatever it was that needed to be handled and hurry back to paradise.

While everyone was packing their things, José, Kane and Big Country were in a private room, discussing future transactions and "what if's" just in case something happened. They knew with mayor Rooney dead and out of the picture, it was going to take time to regain full control of the city. Even though Kane was the city's councilman, his connections had come from dealing with Mayor Rooney.

While sitting down at the table and enjoying breakfast, the three men had come to an understanding.

"Kane, *papi,* listen. You are now the new 'Mayor Rooney'. We got you into that position for a reason, and now it's time to make sure it was worth it. There are a lot of things going on, and you have to get back to South Carolina so you can handle them. I've told you that only the strong survive, and to trust no one. Even though you and your man are the best of friends, you can't even trust him, or him trust you. You never know when one of you will be looking down the barrel of each other's gun. So, keep that in mind. You never know who you may have to kill to get to the next level on your way to the top."

"You right, José. But me and my man right here are bigger than that. Trust me on that."

"Kane, you don't know how many times I have heard that. But let me ask you a question: If I needed someone killed, would you have a problem handling it?"

"I'd handle it without a problem José. The job would get done."

"Well, one thing is for sure. I know you will kill when it's time to. But what if it was out of the blue... a person you cared about?"

"It wouldn't matter. I'm 'bout my business, fam."

"I want you to remember those words. The jet is being refueled, and my pilots have orders to fly you directly to the private airstrip at Anderson Airport. There will be a couple of trucks there waiting for you. There will be a yellow envelope with the information you will need to handle your biz. Just do me a favor."

"What's that, *papi*?"

"Just be a man of your word, and be careful!"

"Will do."

As the three men got up, shook hands and said their goodbyes, José kept his eyes on Big Country. He didn't like his whole demeanor while he was talking to Kane. José was a good judge of character, and had been in the game too long not to know Big Country's type. He knew for the right price, he would kill Kane.

After Kane and Big Country exited the room, José shut the door behind them and remained in his private office as they made their way downstairs. But before they could get all the way down, they were rudely interrupted by a female's voice.

Kane stopped dead in his tracks as soon as he heard Isabella's voice. When she called his name, he already knew what time it was. "Big Country, grab our things and meet me in the lobby."

"Oh yeah, big homie? That's how you doing it now? You on some solo shit?"

"Nah, nothing like that, big homie. You know that's

José's niece, and she looks out for us when he ain't around."

"Yeah? That's a good reason to fuck the connect's niece!"

"Cuz, stop trippin'! I'm right behind you." Kane wasn't sure, but after that crazy conversation in José's office, he made a mental note to start keeping a closer eye on Big Country. He didn't like the vibe that he had just gotten from him. It seemed like there was a little envy and jealousy hidden in it.

As soon as Kane reached the bedroom door, Isabella snatched him into the room and started tugging and pulling on his pants. Dropping down to her knees, she didn't even give him a chance to attempt to stop her. She had his dick out and in her mouth before he could say anything. *"Slurp-slurp-smack!"* were the only sounds in the room as she swallowed and sucked.

Enjoying every second, Kane knew he couldn't resist her and her sex. He just gave in, and moved her beautiful jet black hair to the side with one hand while holding the back of her head with his other hand. He locked eyes with her as he guided her up and down his dick.

Isabella knew what he liked, and was going to make sure he enjoyed every suck and lick that she could give.

Biting on his bottom lip, he just stared as she opened her bathrobe, slid her hand between her legs and started rubbing her stash box until it got moist enough for her to start finger-fucking herself. With one hand, she stroked his dick back and forth, and with her other hand, she took the juices from herself and rubbed it all over his dick as she kept sucking on it.

Isabella was no stranger to swallowing his cum, but this time she wanted it all over her body. Feeling his vein throbbing in her mouth, she knew he was almost ready. She stood up and pulled him towards her bed.

Kane knew he didn't have enough time to hit it like she wanted him to, so he tried to stop her. "Isabella, baby, we don't have enough time for this."

"Yes, *papi,* I know we don't. But for what I want, we do. I want your cum all over me. I want to taste it. I want to rub it all over my stomach and face. Come here. I want to do something new."

Kane didn't know what to expect, but he was willing to try whatever it was she wanted to do, as long as he didn't have to fuck her and get all sweaty.

Sitting on the bed, Isabella put both hands between her legs and massaged her clit until her juices starting flowing into the palms of her hands. Once she felt that she had enough cum in her hands, she took them and placed them around his dick and started rubbing and stroking him until he was fully lubricated. Then, she put him back in her mouth. Pulling, stroking and sucking like crazy, she felt his vein throbbing and knew that it was time. "Hold it, *papi!* Don't cum yet!"

Holding his cum back for as long as he could, Kane watched as she lay back on her bed, placed her feet on his dick and started jerking him off. At first he didn't know what to say, but he didn't stop her. He just stood there with his hands on his hips as if he was superman and Isabella was Louis Lane jerking him off. His facial expression told a story of excitement as he watched her jerking him off with her feet. Squeezing her titties with one hand and fingering herself with her other had really turned him on.

"Yes, *papi!* Now! I'm ready for you!"

When he finally shot off, she sat up with her mouth open and tongue out, catching the first stream of cum on her face. Then she lay back as the rest landed on her breasts and stomach. After smearing it all over herself, she sat up and kissed him before letting him leave.

Chapter 29

As the plane came to a stop, Kane was looking out of the window, watching as the doors to Hangar 5 closed behind the private jet he was in. He noticed the two black trucks and the U-Haul that José told him about.

Everyone was quiet, and knew the seriousness of what was about to happen.

As the door on the jet opened and the stairs were let down, two women walked over and greeted Kane as he stepped off the plane.

"Excuse me, Sir. *Senor* José gave us instructions to escort you to the second truck, and to inform you that everything you need to know is in the glove compartment. He will call you if there is anything else that you need to know."

Kane climbed into the truck and opened the glove compartment to retrieve the yellow envelope.

Big Country told JB and E-Dubb to take the U-Haul and head to the butcher shop. Then, he whispered to Kim that she was to take the other black truck and head to her house. After she dropped the other females off, she, Kwantie and Giovanni were to meet the rest of the crew at the butcher shop.

As everyone pulled off, Big Country jumped into the truck with Kane, and watched as Kane stared blankly out of the window.

Their attention was quickly interrupted by the sound of the truck's phone ringing. Looking around, they weren't sure at first where the noise was coming from until Kane noticed the symbol of a phone on the steering wheel and decided to press it.

"This is Tonya Wilson, reporting live for Channel 6 News."

"We are at a storage facility on Old Airport Road, where police have been tipped off about foul play in one of the storage bins. They were told that storage bin 229 seems to have a red substance leaking from under its gate. The owner of the facility reported seeing it early this morning after making her rounds. She said she tried calling the renter of the bin, but the number was disconnected. She said she then called the police."

"We are here live as the police are now bringing a pair of bolt cutters to cut the lock. It appears that they have a search warrant and permission from the facility's owner. Ladies and gentlemen, there is no telling what is behind the gate..."

As the cameraman zoomed in on the gate, the viewers were wondering themselves. As the gate went up, there was silence. Tonya Wilson's mouth dropped, as if she was at a loss for words.

> *"Oh my God! Those are human remains in the storage bin! Ladies and gentlemen, this is not fake. This is live coverage. I'm not sure, but it seems like they were murdered, and the bodies were just left here! Zoom in! Zoom in! Hurry up and get a shot of this before they close the gate!"*

The cameraman zoomed in as close he could. He was trying to get a close-up of each of the victims. Moving his camera around and trying to catch different angles, the camera froze on the last man's face. "What da fuck! Tonya, it's the mayor!"

"What? Who did you say?"

"It's muthafuckin' Mayor Rooney!"

Tonya couldn't believe her eyes. All four men were bound and gagged, with bullet holes in their bodies and in their heads.

> *"Ladies and gentlemen, I apologize for the gruesome sight that we have just shown you. We were not expecting to see anything of the sort..."*
>
> *"Cut! Go to commercial!"*

The news station cut from the live broadcast.

Due to who was in that storage bin, the stakes were higher, and everyone was fair game as of that moment. The authorities knew that if someone would take out half of the police task force and kill the mayor, they meant business.

"Hello, may I speak to a Miss Palico?"

"Yes, this is she. How may I help you?"

"Ma'am, this is the Anderson Police Department, and your number was listed as the next of kin for a Mrs. Rooney."

"Yes."

"Are you with her right now?"

"No. What is going on? Is everything okay?"

"Ma'am, her husband, Mayor Rooney has just been found dead inside of a storage bin out on Old Airport Road."

"No! Please don't tell me that! Are you sure?"

"Ma'am, as bad as I wish it was a joke, it's not."

"Well, thank you. I'll break the news to her."

"Got-damn it, Mitch! Where the fuck have you been? Man, I'm as hungry as a boatload of starving Africans that have been at sea for four months!"

"Calm the fuck down, Thomas. I've been at the department, checking out what the fuck is going on."

"Hell, you're acting like I'm the damn hostage or something! Shit! You're starving me like I did something to you. So, what the fuck did you come up with?"

"First off, our boss, Captain 'Dickhead' has allowed the feds to come in and help with the investigation. They've got some super cop bitch running the show. She's a sexy ass white bitch too. But anyway, Captain Dickhead has shut the streets down."

"Secondly, they just found Mayor Rooney dead in some damn storage bin with two Spanish men. And get this; they also found the body of Cashmere Woodson in there with them."

"Man, stop bullshitting me! Cashmere Woodson? Oh my God! Who the fuck would kill Cashmere and Mayor Rooney?"

"Thomas, that 'who' has to be Kane."

"Get the fuck outta here! Why would Kane kill his own brother and Mayor Rooney? What would he have to gain?"

"Look. With Cashmere gone and Mayor Rooney dead, Kane could take over the city with no problem. Who better than the city's councilman himself?"

"Hello, *papi*. I see y'all made it safely. You got the information out of the glove compartment yet?"

"Yeah, I got everything."

"A'ight, Kane. I'll call you later. Just remember, only the dirtiest players survive in this game. The deeper you get, the more people will begin to hate you. *Papi*, my name tells the story, just like that big Spanish rapper from the Bronx whose name his CD J.O.S.E.—Jealous Ones Still Envy. Always keep that in mind. Get the streets in order and get the fuck out of there. Handle your business, and you'll be able to take the whole summer off.

Kane walked into JB's Butcher Shop through the back door without anyone noticing him. Once he reached the back room where everyone was waiting for him, he just stood there and stared at all of their blank expressions.

"Listen. We are here for two things, and two things only. José has given us the dope to flood the streets with. But, we are also here for Shawn. Our main focus is to get

Carp back."

"We have more dope than we can handle, but Big Country will take care of all that. Y'all already know the deal and how to handle y'alls' business. Please, everyone be careful. The same people that are sitting here right now are the same people I want to be leaving here with. This is the new family."

Before Kane could finish, Shawn knocked on the door and came in with the evilest look a human could have. The room fell silent as they watched and listened to him tell the story of what happened to his father and how he was kidnapped. No one said a word until he had finished. Everyone could feel his pain.

"Listen up, everyone. Here are the pictures of the two cops that kidnapped Shawn's father."

Out of everyone looking at the pictures, Kim stared at them the hardest. They were the same two cops that came into the house the night that Jason was murdered, and the same two white cops they saw in the truck parked at the club.

Everyone sat and listened as Kane laid out the format of the plan. He was precise about what he wanted done. He made sure that everyone knew their part before he finished and moved on to the next phase of the plan. He wanted his whole crew to be on their P's and Q's and not miss a beat.

Cindy walked into Mrs. Rooney's room at Anderson Memorial Hospital, carrying flowers and balloons in one hand and some food from the restaurant across the street from the hospital in the other. But she had gotten there too late. Mrs. Rooney was already in tears. Looking at Mrs.

Rooney, she could tell that she already knew about her husband.

The silence was broken by Mrs. Rooney. "It's okay, Cindy. I know, sweetheart. It's been all over the news. Trust me, I'm okay. At least now I know."

"I'm so sorry, Mrs. Rooney. Is there anything I can do for you?"

"Don't be sorry, Cindy. I knew what kind of lifestyle my husband was living, so I'm not surprised by the way he died. I'm more surprised that it didn't happen a lot sooner. He was good to me, but he was still a piece of shit. But, he was *my* piece of shit."

"Mrs. Rooney, you don't have to talk about it right now."

"You're right. But there's no need for sorrow. Let's eat so I can take my nap."

"Kane, what are we waiting for?"

"Ain't no one leaving until this fucking phone rings. Until then, we're just gonna sit here and wait for those two white muthafuckers to call."

Chapter 30

"Splash!"

The ice cold water woke Carp instantly. Still blindfolded, he couldn't see a thing. He had lost count of the hours and minutes. What had only been a few days felt like an eternity. He could hear faint voices in the other room, so he knew that he wasn't alone. Remaining quiet, he knew that there were at least two other people in the house.

"Thomas, what are we gonna do with this piece of shit nigger? I'm tired of babysitting his ass."

"Mitch, you act like it's been forever. Damn! It's only been a couple of hours. Let me see your phone."

"Hello. Who is this?"

"That's not important. If you ever want to see Carp alive again, you need to follow these instructions: First, you need to get in touch with Kane Woodson and have him answer your phone the next time I call."

"Yo, who is Kane Wood—"

Before Shawn could finish his question, Thomas had hung up the cell phone.

Carp heard the entire conversation and was praying that whoever was on the other end of the line could be of help. Time was of the essence. He hoped that the person knew that every second counted right now.

As soon as the phone went dead, everyone was staring at Shawn. He repeated the message out loud before handing Kane the phone.

After hearing the message, Kane was totally pissed off. He didn't take kindly to threats, especially ones coming from crooked ass white cops. Fuel was added to the fire, and it had awakened the monster that they should have left sleeping. He didn't expect that being at the top was so hard, but in life, nothing came easy.

He got up, walked over to the wall and had JB punch a code into a keypad. The entire side wall slid open, and the hidden room was full of artillery. Everyone except Giovanni got up and grabbed the weapon of their choice.

Watching closely, Giovanni finally got up and followed suit. Her choice of gun was a Glock-40.

Kwantie grabbed the standard police issue Glock 9-mm, while Kim grabbed her new favorites, two Glock 380's and a snub nose revolver with no hammer.

Country was staring at Kwantie, and couldn't figure out why she would grab a police gun. He wondered if it was instinctive, or if she just didn't know any better. He made a mental note to watch her every move.

As everyone was grabbing their guns, Kane reached into his pocket and pulled out his wallet. While looking at the picture of his parents, he noticed a piece of folded up paper barely sticking out behind it. Remembering that Mrs. Rooney said not to open it until she contacted him, he pushed it back behind the picture and closed his wallet back up.

"Kane, you a'ight, homie? You look a little puzzled."

"Nah, Country, I'm good. I was just thinking about going to Mrs. Rooney."

"I feel you, dawg. I could go for some of that vanilla ice cream. It's been a minute since I hit that little secretary up."

"Country, make sure that everybody handles their business today. Have JB deliver all the coke to the stash spots so they can get started. Them niggas in the streets are beginning to starve. I'm 'bout to slide for a quick minute and go see Angela. I'll get with you later."

After everyone got themselves situated, they all left in separate cars, except for Kim and Kwantie. They had other plans before handling their street business. They weren't upset with Kane for having Giovanni participate in their private sex-capades on the Island, but they wanted to be alone and enjoy each other.

While Kim was driving, Kwantie lifted Kim's skirt and buried her face between her legs. Rubbing her head, Kim was enjoying the moment of pleasure at the red light.

Leaning her head back, Kim lifted her leg up and put it over Kwantie's shoulder. Licking and fingering Kim so fast had caused Kim to close her eyes and enjoy every second of it, until the light had changed green and the other cars started honking their horns.

Not giving a damn, Kim started humping Kwantie's face as the other cars began to go around them. Kim had made her mind up, and was not stopping Kwantie until she came. The light turned red once again before she started shaking. She lifted her shirt up and started rubbing and squeezing her breasts as Kwantie kept pushing her fingers in and out of her secret juice box. Biting her bottom lip, Kim held Kwantie's head while her juices started gushing out. By the time the light turned green again, they were smiling at each other when the cars started honking their horns again and going around them.

Kwantie knew that as soon as she got her chance, Kim was going to get her back. But it was time to hit the streets and get that paper.

"Mr. Woodson! What are you doing up here?"

"Hey, Cindy! I'm coming to see a friend. Then I was going to see if I could sneak in and see my baby."

"Well, I'm on my way back to her room. I'll let her know that you're here and that you'll be stopping by."

"You don't have to do that. I want to surprise her. Plus, I heard that the Secret Service is around, so I don't need anyone else to know I'm here. A'ight?"

"Yeah, you're right. I'll see you in a few. Kane, where is my baby?"

"Who, Country? Don't worry, he's a'ight. He was just talking about seeing you."

"Well, tell him that I think I'm falling in love."

"Girl, you're crazy! I'll see you in a few minutes."

As Kane rounded the corner, Angela stepped out of the elevator and their eyes met. She got weak instantly. She didn't know what it was about him, but every time he came around she would get moist.

Walking towards her, Kane started smiling. Angela

was licking her lips with every step she took. He grabbed her by the waist and they embraced and started kissing. "Baby, I want you right now!" he said.

"Kane, I'm on duty. I'm running the floor right now."

"So what? You telling me no?"

"No. No, baby. I want you too, but I have to make my rounds. Come. Walk with me."

Kane didn't hesitate. They went to about ten rooms. The last room was empty, and as soon as they stepped in, he pushed Angela back to the door and unbuttoned her white coat. While kissing her, he was rubbing her breasts. From kissing, he went to licking and sucking on her neck.

Angela started breathing heavily as he slid his hand into her scrub pants. Feeling the moistness, he slid two fingers inside of her with ease. She let out a loud, uncontrollable moan.

Looking in her eyes, Kane got down on his knees and pulled down her pants and panties to expose her freshly shaven vagina. Pulling one leg out of her pants, he placed her leg over his shoulder and began to make love to her with his mouth.

Unable to take the pleasure, she started grinding on his face to the rhythm of his tongue.

Once he felt her body tense up, he stopped and immediately took her to a gurney. He climbed on top and lay on his back. Angela then climbed on top of him and began to ride him. With her hands on his chest, she grinded and lifted her hips in a circular motion, causing him to grab her waist and bury himself deeper. Still with her white coat on, she was moving her hips like a snake. Unable to stand the pressure that was building up, she laid down on his chest while Kane kept pumping inside of her until the moistness went from wet to creamy.

Moaning without a care in the world, Angela didn't

care if anyone walked in at this point. She just enjoyed having sex with Kane.

As she was getting up, Kane was smiling while looking at her body. "Damn! You're so muthafuckin' sexy, baby! You're gonna make me fall in love with your ass, Angela."

"Kane, you need to stop it! You don't have to lie to me. No matter what happens between us, I'll always love you, a'ight?"

"Angela, I'm not playing. I'm dead ass serious. Baby girl, the whole time I was gone I was thinking about you. Me and Country were talking about you, and he kept telling me that you're the one for me."

"What did you say?"

"I agreed. I truly believe that you are the one, and I want to give us a chance, if you're willing to give me a chance."

"Kane, you're gonna make me cry. I do truly love you and I hope you are serious, because I am, and there's nothing I wouldn't do for you, baby."

As they cleaned up and got dressed, Angela's pager went off, alerting her of an emergency in the ER. She turned and kissed Kane, and hurried out of the room.

Kane had given some thought as to what he had just done. He had a long conversation with Big Country about Angela. Kane was far from stupid, and he was looking at the bigger picture. Angela had a good job, nice house, a car and good benefits. It was worth taking a chance with her. He knew he couldn't be with Kim and Kwantie for the rest of his life. It was cool to have some freaky shit going on, but at some point in his life he wanted the American dream. He knew he wanted a family.

Angela had one child—a little girl—and Kane had none. Time was closing in on him. He wanted to be able to play with his kids before he was too old.

"Hey Cindy, how's she doing?"

"Cindy, who is that?"

"Mrs. Rooney, it's your baby."

When Cindy stepped to the side, Mrs. Rooney's eyes opened wide and a smile came across her face like she was in heaven. She reached up to hug Kane. Once they touched, her eyes teared up instantly. "Cindy, could you please give us a few minutes?"

Before the door closed all the way, Mrs. Rooney had her tongue down Kane's throat and one hand on his dick. "Baby, I miss you so much! I know my husband is dead and I know you had something to do with it, but that doesn't matter to me, because I'm in love with you and I want to be with you. I know it will be hard for us, but we can make it."

"Baby, nothing is what it seems," she continued. "I know you think that you were working for my husband, but you really were working for me. Even my husband was working for me."

"The man you know as José, he's my half-brother. We have the same mother. My mother left his father and left the island to get away from his family, and that's how she ended up in South Carolina. When she got here, she met a white guy who she fell in love with. That's why I look more white than Hispanic. But José found me when we got older. I've been flooding the southeast with cocaine for the longest. I'm sorry you had to find out this way, but I wanted to be the one to tell you. I apologize, baby."

Kane was stunned and didn't know what to think. He couldn't believe what he was hearing and was at a loss for words. As he stared at her, she begged him not to say anything to José, because he would have both of them killed. This was a secret that she was supposed to take to her grave.

"Hey, girl! I miss you, baby! When you get this message, call me back. It's been a long time. Call me at the house." Cindy hung up the phone. It had been a few months since she last talked to her baby. The longer they stayed apart, the deeper her feelings became for a man. She was beginning to get upset with her partner/lover for not responding to her calls.

"Is this Kane Woodson?"

"Yeah. What da fuck do you want wit' me?"

"Shut the fuck up and listen, nigger! If you want to see Carp's black ass alive again, you will have one million dollars by tomorrow night."

"Where am I supposed to get that type of cash from, cracker?"

"That's not my problem. You just get the fucking money. I'll call you back tomorrow at twelve to give you the location where to bring it."

The phone went dead. Kane sat in the truck, plotting his next move when his phone rang. "Yo, what's up?"

"Hey, *papi!* How are things going?"

"Let's just say that everything is almost back to normal. José, where is the other information you were telling me about?"

"Look under the driver's seat. Remember, through

blood sweat and tears, nothing is what it appears. I'm not worried about Shawn telling on us, but the other person in the picture could cause us major problems. She has to be disposed of."

"Don't worry, José. I'll handle it... whoever and whatever it is. Oh yeah. One of those two cops called. I'm supposed to wait for another call tomorrow night at twelve for further instructions. They want a million."

"Listen. There's no way possible I can get to the States on such short notice, but I can send you some real soldiers. As far as the money goes, go ahead and give 'em what they want, and I'll take care of you on the back end. But do what you have to do if you can pull it off without giving up the money. Make sure the exterminators that I send you kill all of the rodents this time. I'm sending two of my people tonight. I'll have them contact you when they arrive."

"A'ight. Well, I'm 'bout to check this info out and handle my biz. I'll hit you back when your people get here."

Chapter 31

While Kim went into the store, Kwantie was checking her messages. She had so much going on that she forgot to check them. She was using the business phone that Kane had given her. After reading one of the messages, she got nervous and hung up when she saw Kim coming out of the store.

Country had dropped all of the cocaine off and was on his way back to JB's Butcher Shop when he saw Giovanni coming out of a corner store. Instead of turning the corner, he pulled into the store's parking lot and parked a few cars down from hers. Waiting and watching her, he decided to follow her.

Giovanni never realized that she was being followed. During the entire drive to her house, she was contemplating on her next move. When she got home, she even failed to notice the car that had parked a few houses down from hers. So caught up in what she was thinking, she got out of the car and went straight into the house.

Country was determined to find out what was going on with this chick. He didn't have time to call Kane. When the lights went on in the front part of the house, he waited for her next move.

Opening the envelope that was under the seat, Kane was not expecting to see what he was looking at. He was looking at Mrs. Rooney's face in the picture. At the bottom was a little note that read:

> *Whatever and however, please don't make it messy. She is my only sister, and I want to at least give her a proper burial.*

"Got-damn it! Shit! What da fuck! Mrs. Rooney? Damn! That's my baby! She wasn't lying to me. Got-damn it! Nothing is what it appears to be!"

Thinking out loud, Kane was hitting the steering wheel, upset with himself and José. Kane had never been in a situation where he had to think twice about something.

Kane was sitting in the hospital parking lot, wondering how he could get back upstairs when he saw Cindy coming out of the side door. Looking at her while she was walking in his direction and talking on her cell phone, he flashed his lights to get her attention.

Cindy was caught off guard when the bright lights hit her. She recognized Kane's truck and quickly finished her conversation. After she got into the truck and sat down, she said, "Hey, Kane. You alright? You look like you've been crying. You okay, honey?"

"Yeah, Cindy, I'm good. I was just thinking about ol' girl upstairs."

"Kane, she's gonna be alright. You know she's a fighter. You don't have to worry."

"Cindy, we're cool and everything, but I don't let women call me 'honey' if we ain't fucking and we ain't done that… yet."

"Oh my God! Where did that come from? Because if I wanted to, I could have had you. I figured that you were too afraid to cheat on Mrs. Rooney. But to be honest with you, I've always wanted to. I know I've messed with Country, but I used to imagine you inside me when he and I were having sex."

"Cut the bullshit, Cindy! 'Cause if you wanted this, you could have gotten it. But you fuck with my man, Country, and I don't rock like that."

"Rock like what?"

Before Kane could answer, she had unzipped his pants and put his dick in her mouth. He tried to stop her, but it happened so fast. Bobbing her head up and down while stroking him caused Kane to let the seat back and enjoy the moment.

Feeling the throbbing in her mouth, she looked Kane in the eyes and started moving her hand and head up and down faster. The friction caused him to explode in her mouth without warning. It didn't matter whether he gave her a warning or not. She swallowed every drop of his juices anyway.

Kane thought that it was over, but Cindy slid her pants down, climbed on top of Kane and straddled him while he was laid back in the driver's seat. Gripping his manhood, she slowly placed it in her and began grinding.

While they stared into each other's eyes, Kane unbuttoned her silk blouse, exposing her breasts. Her breasts were perfect, and had the pinkest nipples. He leaned up and placed one in his mouth while palming and fondling the other one.

R. Kelly's "Seems Like You're Ready" was coming through the speakers as Cindy rode him like a horse in a rodeo. His moans excited her so much that she started going all the way up and slamming back down on him.

When the phone started ringing, Kane didn't really want to answer it, but he knew he had no choice. While reaching between the seats, he felt what he thought was a gun under Cindy's pants, but he wasn't sure. Still reaching a little further, he finally got to his phone. "What's up Big Country?"

"Yo, I followed that bitch, Giovanni. I'm outside of her crib right now. Damn, cuz! What's dat noise in da background?"

"Man, I'm up here at the hospital."

"Oh, you up there hitting Angela, huh?"

"Nah, homie. I got this white chick I just met, and the pussy is fire, my nigga! I might have to keep this one for myself."

"I feel ya. But if anything pops off, I'll get at you."

Kane hurried and hung up the phone so he could get back into what he and Cindy were doing. While he was on the phone, she didn't stop riding him, even though she knew that he was talking to Country.

As soon as he hung up the phone, he turned and laid her on her back. He put her legs on top of his shoulders and gave her what she wanted. The moans turned to screams of pleasure before they both were out of breath and tired.

As they started getting dressed, Kane couldn't wait to ask, "Cindy, what da fuck did we just do?"

"I don't know, but trust me, I enjoyed all of it! You don't have to worry about your boy getting anymore of these goods…You could turn a gay bitch straight! I'm serious!"

"Whatever, Cindy. I can't front though. I didn't think you were as good as you were. You surprised me."

"I'm full of surprises, boo. I can call you that now, right?"

"Yes, I guess I'm your honey. Can I ask you one more question? What are you doing with a gun?"

"Mitch, give me a hand. This nigger is heavy. We have to put his ass in the van. Come on, partner. We're about to be rich. This is the meal ticket that we've been waiting for our entire career."

"Thomas, when this is over I'm going to get my family and get the fuck out of this little ass town. What about you?"

"I'm going to Vegas. After that, I don't know. But I promise that I won't be working for anyone else, Mitch."

"Yeah, I hear you. Let's get going so we can make sure the parking lot is clear when we make the exchange."

"Kane, don't ask questions that you're not ready to hear the answers to."

"Fuck you mean by that? What, you some kind of secretary/assassin or something?"

"If I was, what would you do?"

"To tell you the truth, I'd be forced to kill your ass."

"Well, as far as the gun goes, if I wanted you dead, you would've been dead. But after tonight and what we just did and how you made me feel, I'd let you go just because of that good ass dick you got. Plus, if you eat pussy just as good, I'd marry your ass! But we'd have to get rid of Country, because there is no way I'm going to be around two men I've had had sex with, especially if I'm married to one of them. That wouldn't be fair to me or you. Also, just remember, don't judge a book by its cover. Nothing is what it seems in life.

"Yo, what da fuck did you just say? I've heard dat shit 'bout three or four times today."

"Well, you should be following that advice. But anyway, I'll catch you later!"

As Cindy got out of the truck, Kane couldn't help but to watch the white woman sashay across the parking lot. He couldn't begin to believe what had just happened. Cindy was thick for a white woman. Her body was fine and toned. He could tell that she took care of herself. He really didn't have love for white women, but she was the type that he would like to have for himself. He had put it on her so good that he forgot about Big Country. But in the game, José told him that only the dirtiest players survive.

Watching Cindy, he thought about a line from the movie, "Heat":

"...If you can't walk away from what you love in thirty seconds, you don't need to be in this game..."

Those words stayed with him every day, and was the main reason why he had never settled down. But Angela—and now Cindy had blown his mind. Kane knew he was slipping, and had to catch himself. He thought about it for a few more seconds and shook it off.

He grabbed his gun, cocked it and chambered one of the bullets, jumped out of the truck and walked back towards the hospital while screwing the silencer on.

"What's up? May I speak to Kim? Kane told me to call this number when I needed something."

"This is Kim. Who's dis, and what do you want?"

"Slow down, lil' mama! This is Blac. I need two of them things. I'm up by the store on Whitner Street. How long you gonna be?"

"I'll be there in ten minutes. What are you in?"

"A powder blue Benz."

When Kim got back in the car, Kwantie was acting suspicious, but Kim said nothing. She made a mental note to keep an eye on her as they pulled off.

"Where we headed, Kim?"

"I'm going to the eastside to drop these two bricks off with Blac."

"Blac? When did Blac start hanging on the east side? He used to be on the west side, copping from Cash all the time."

"Well, Kwantie, if the nigga tries anything stupid, his ass dies. We're gonna have to put our mark down out here in these streets to let muthafuckers know not to try us."

"I'm with you, baby. You know I'm with you 'til the end."

On the way over to the east side, Kwantie cocked and put a bullet in the chambers of both of their guns. She had a funny feeling about the situation and wanted to be ready if anything popped off. Reaching in the back seat, she grabbed the two bulletproof vests and handed one to Kim.

While sitting at the red light on Main Street, they both put their vests on and made sure that they were on snug and tight. Leaning over, Kim kissed Kwantie on the lips and smiled. The light turned green and they pulled off. Not knowing what to expect, they were prepared to do whatever it took to survive.

Kim was a good girl who had been turned out by the streets, and she had no intentions of ever turning back. She was too far gone and couldn't turn back if she wanted to. She was now part of the fam.

Before they knew it, they were driving down Whitner Street. Kim pulled over to let Kwantie out before driving up to the store. As Kim was pulling into the parking lot, she quickly noticed that the street lights were out, but the lights on the store's sign were bright enough for her to see her surroundings.

Kim didn't know what Blac looked like, but Kwantie had described him as best she could. Looking in the rearview mirror, she saw Blac coming across the street with a book bag over his shoulder. As she continued to look around, she wasn't sure if she saw movement on the side of the store.

Walking through the parking lot, Kwantie had on a dark hoody, and no one paid her any attention. She made her way to the side of the store, where even she thought that she had seen some shady shit going on. Once on the side of the store, she pretended to use the phone so she could have a clear view of Kim and the car.

When Blac got up to the car, he told Kim that he wanted to see the dope before he gave up the money. She smiled and told him that she wanted to see the money first.

Blac walked around to the passenger side of the car and got in.

Kwantie was still watching, but acting like she was arguing with her boyfriend over the phone.

"Yo, what's up, lil' mama? This is what Kane is working with now? You the Queen Bitch of the east side?

You the one that's gonna be running Cash's shit now, huh?"

Blac was talking too much shit. He was so used to dealing with Cash that he forgot that the east side was run by Jason, and not Cash. His last statement immediately grabbed her attention. Even though she didn't say anything, she had been with Jason enough times to know that Cash had no control over the east side. She became suspicious and started reading his body language the way that Kane had taught her.

Kim wasn't about to take a chance. She tried to reach under her lap and grab her 38 snub nose while she was reaching for the two bricks of cocaine under the seat. When she came up with the bag, she noticed two men with hoody's on coming out of the store, and each one held a brown paper bag with their hand in it. She was also trying to watch Blac, as the two hooded men came up to the car and tapped on the window with their guns pointed directly at her face.

"Bitch, you know what it is. Let us get the shit with no problem and you'll live. As a matter of fact, let the got-damn window down."

"I can't. It's broke."

When Kim turned her head back around, Blac had his gun pointed at her face with a devilish grin. "You know what it is, bitch. A nigga's hungry out here."

"So, after all these years, you gonna try and rob Kane like that?"

"Tell that nigga I said fuck him! Him and Country can suck my dick! Now, give me the other bag."

By this time, Kwantie had peeped game and had dropped the phone and started walking towards the car.

Chapter 32

Heading up in the elevator, Kane was determined to handle his business. Nothing was ever personal in his life. Even though he really enjoyed having sex with Mrs. Rooney, he knew business was business. Plus, he had already given José his word on handling his situation. It was an order that had to be carried out.

When the elevator came to a stop and the doors opened, Kane saw Cindy headed in the opposite direction from Mrs. Rooney's room. He didn't hesitate for one second.

When he got to the door, he peeked his head in the room to see if Mrs. Rooney was alone. Once he saw the room was clear, he stepped in and closed the door behind him as quietly as he could, trying not to alert her to his presence.

"Kane! Hey, baby! I knew you'd be back. Baby, trust me when I say I love you, and you will be a part of me, and I will be a part of you forever. When you get back in your truck, open up the letter I gave you. Baby, please don't cry. You will be a great leader."

Kane watched and listened as the tears fell from his eyes. He noticed at that point how fine she really was. She was thicker than he was used to seeing her. She sat up and kissed him on the lips and wiped his tears.

While hugging him, she never saw it coming. Kane shot her twice in the chest, and laid her down and shut her eyes before getting up and walking out of the room as if nothing happened.

After slamming the car door, Blac turned to run and froze in his tracks when he saw the two 9mm Glocks pointed at his face.

"Bitch ass nigga, what did you tell her to tell my man? To suck your dick? Nah. How about you suck this!"

The first gunshot caused Blac to drop to his knees and grab what was left of his dick. Looking up at Kwantie, he watched as she walked up on him and put the barrel in his mouth. The heat from the barrel burned his lips enough to make him moan out loud. He heard one of his hooded homeboys yell, "Yo, let him go, bitch, before we spray your girl!"

Kim looked out of the window at the two hooded men and started to laugh at them. While the smaller of the two men kept his aim on her, the taller one pointed his gun at Kwantie. But it was too late. Kwantie had one gun in Blac's mouth and another one pointed at them.

When Kim started laughing, the smaller of the two didn't hesitate. He squeezed the trigger and fired into the driver side window. The first shot startled Kwantie so badly that she unintentionally shot Blac in the face, scattering his brains all over the side of the car and in the parking lot.

The taller of the two men started shooting at Kwantie, but his aim was so bad that he couldn't hit her if she was standing two feet in front of him. Kwantie snapped out of her daze and fired back as she ran closer to the car for cover.

The dude that was shooting at Kim realized that the window was bulletproof. But by the time he did, it was too late because he was out of bullets. Dropping his gun, he turned and took off running.

Kwantie peeked over the car and let off two quick shots, hitting him in the leg. Forgetting about the second hooded man hiding behind the car, she never saw him creep up behind her.

Kim was smiling when the first dude running across the parking lot got hit and fell. By the time she turned to look at Kwantie, her face froze with fear. She also forgot about the other hooded gunmen.

Kwantie looked through the windshield of the car to make sure that Kim was okay, and saw fear on Kim's face. All she could do was turn around and hope that God was with her tonight. But before she knew it, the other man had gotten two quick shots off.

Kim was out of the car with the quickness, and took aim on the man. The first shot hit him in the shoulder and spun him around. The second shot hit him in the neck, and the third hit him in the chest, leaving him for dead.

Kim was scared shitless. She didn't see Kwantie until she ran all the way around the car. Kwantie was stretched out on the ground, holding her chest.

"Bitch, don't just stand there! Help a bitch get in the car so we can get the fuck out of here!"

"Kwantie, you scared the shit out of me, bitch!" Kim didn't waste any time helping Kwantie get into the car. As she was about to pull out of the parking lot, she saw the first gunman who was shot in the leg, crawling away in her rearview mirror. Kim put the car in reverse and ran over his ass. Once she had cleared his body, she slammed the car in park, jumped out and shot him in the face until her revolver was empty. But she still wasn't done. She jumped back in the car and ran him over again before finally leaving the parking lot.

The two women left a very nasty first impression on the streets. They were not to be fucked with, and they demanded respect just like any man in the game.

Country got out of the car and made his way to the side of the house. Looking through the window had made him feel like a peeping Tom, but he was on a mission. Giovanni had stripped down to her panties and bra and was walking around her bedroom.

Country had been looking through the window for quite some time. He had grown tired and was debating whether or not he should knock on the door. Continuing to watch her, she made her way to the bathroom. Unable to see, he waited a few more minutes before walking to the front door. He figured that she was in the shower or taking a bath, so he picked the lock and entered her house.

He was impressed by the décor. She was living like a real live baller. Looking around, he was trying to find anything out of the ordinary.

Seeing the pictures on the curio shelf, he looked at them to see if he recognized anybody. Before he turned and walked away, there was a picture that caught his eye.

In it, Giovanni was hugging a white woman who looked so familiar to him. The picture had distracted him for so long that he didn't hear the water turn off in the bathroom. He was still staring at the picture, trying to remember who the female with Giovanni was.

"Country, what da fuck are you doing in my house? I don't remember inviting your ass in here. Does Kane know you're here?"

"Yeah, he knows. But that's not important right now. What's important is your ass, and who you are. You might have the rest of them fooled, but I know something ain't right about you."

"What are you saying? You think I'm a cop or something? If I was, do you really think a cop would be in a strip club, butt naked and dancing and fucking for a living? Do you think a cop would be lying up with two other females while sexing Kane? If I was a cop, would I be standing in my living room with just a towel on, soaking wet? No, I don't think so! And, if I was a cop, would I do this?"

Country couldn't believe his eyes. Giovanni had dropped to her knees, pulled his dick out of his pants and started deep throating him. He just went with the flow and grabbed the back of her head while she swallowed him whole.

Giovanni felt his knees buckle a little, so she got up and pushed him down on the couch. Not giving him a chance to think, she jumped on top of him and started riding him like there was no tomorrow while making all kinds of noises.

Country was turned on. He lifted her up, turned her around, put her on her knees on the couch and started hitting her doggie style.

Giovanni was enjoying every thrust and pump that

Country threw her way. Throwing it back just as hard as she was, caused the both of them to cum at the same time.

They both collapsed onto the couch and were enjoying each other's touch, but Giovanni was enjoying it the most. Besides sleeping with Kane, Kim and Kwantie. She had forgotten the feeling of being with just one man. Turning over to face him, she threw her leg over his and slid him back into her and asked him, "If I was a cop, would you be laid up in my house with your dick up in me, slowly humping and grinding?"

In the hospital parking lot, Kane was sitting in his truck, watching as police cars started pulling up. He already knew that they had found Mrs. Rooney's body. There was no saving her; she had to go. Thinking of her last comment, he reached in his wallet, pulled out the piece of paper she had given him and opened it up:

> *Kane, if you are reading this, I must be dead. I want to apologize for not telling you this earlier. Please understand that I didn't know how to tell you.*
>
> *Baby, I'm eight weeks pregnant. I know it's yours because my husband and I haven't had sex in almost a year.*
>
> *I love you!*

Kane couldn't believe what he had just read. Tears filled his eyes as he sat there and thought about everything that was happening. He had just killed the mother of his firstborn. He knew that he had to leave the parking lot before something else happened. He needed to get to a quiet place where he could think.

Before he could pull out, his phone started ringing.

Seeing the code 007E, he knew it was another emergency. "Kim, what's up? Is everything okay?"

"No, baby. I went to meet Blac on the east side, and he and two other niggas tried to rob Kwantie and me. Kwantie got shot, but she had her vest on so she's okay."

"Blac? You talking 'bout Blac with da power blue Benz? What da fuck was he doing meeting you on the east side? That nigga is from the west side. As a matter of fact, how did he get your number? You know what? Don't even worry about it. I'll handle his ass myself."

"Ain't no need to, unless you plan on going to hell, 'cause me and Kwantie killed all three of their asses. We left them in the middle of the parking lot over on the east side. As far as Blac is concerned, he'll be having a closed casket funeral."

"A'ight then. Y'all meet me at JB's, and be careful. When y'all get there, tell E-Dubb to get rid of the car. We have a couple of hours before we handle the shit with them two crooked ass white cops."

"Good evening. Tonight is the night that this case comes to a close. Mrs. Rooney was murdered right under our noses. The hospital's surveillance system shows Kane Woodson fleeing the scene. We have an A.P.B. out on his whereabouts. If anyone finds him, do not—I repeat—do not try to apprehend him alone. Please call me. Just watch him until we can set up a perimeter and get S.W.A.T. there. Kane Woodson is extremely dangerous. Everyone, let's be safe tonight."

As everyone suited up, Cindy stared at the pictures of Kane and shook her head. She had bad feeling in her gut. Even though she was in love with her partner, she felt like if given a chance, she could change Kane.

"Miss Palico, the dispatcher just radioed and informed us of a shooting at a grocery store on Whitner Street. Do you think that has anything to do with Mr. Woodson?"

"I'm not sure. What are the details?"

"Three men were gunned down in the parking lot. One of them is still alive. He's at the hospital right now, where they're trying to save his life. Witnesses reported that they thought it was a robbery gone bad. But get this; they say it was two women who did the killings."

"Yeah, you need to get over there and check it out. I'm almost certain that Mr. Woodson's crew is behind it, and this time they have finally fucked up. They left somebody alive. Call me when you get something."

Giovanni and Country had just gotten out of the shower and were drying off before getting dressed, when both of their cell phones started ringing. Seeing the 007-#1, they knew it was Kane. Country called first and got the report, and then Giovanni did the same.

Looking at each other, she leaned over and kissed him on his lips before they headed to the front door.

Giovanni turned and ran back into her bedroom and grabbed her bulletproof vest.

Getting into separate cars, he followed her to JB's Butcher Shop.

While in the car, Giovanni wanted to make sure that she had not missed any other calls. Listening to her messages, she became upset when she did not hear the voice that she had been waiting for all day.

Country had snatched the picture off of the curio shelf when Giovanni went back into her bedroom. He was trying his best to remember where he knew the white chick with the short Hallie Berry haircut from. He had to put the picture out of his mind for the time being. He knew that whatever Kane wanted to meet for, it had to be serious, and he wanted to get his mind back on track and stay focused.

"Kane! Yo, what da fuck is going on? They say you killed the mayor's wife. I saw the tape with my own eyes. I saw you leaving the hospital in a hurry."

"Angela, what da fuck are you talking 'bout? I ain't killed nobody. Do you think I'm crazy or something? Baby, listen. I just told you I wanted to be with you, and now you come with this bullshit? You know what? I don't need any more fucking drama in my life right now."

"Baby, wait. I'm sorry. I didn't mean anything by it. I just wanted to make sure it wasn't you. I love you, Kane, and I'll do anything to be with you."

"Anything?"

"Yes, baby. You name it. I won't let you get away from me this time. Just give me a chance to prove my love for you."

"Family, listen to me, and listen good. Tonight, two of us were attacked, and niggas tried to rob them. Thanks to Better Aiming Shooting Gallery, Kim and Kwantie are still here with us. But, on the other hand, we now have three dead men on our hands."

Now here's the important news. First and foremost, the person that José wanted me to kill was his sister, who y'all know was Mrs. Rooney. I went to the hospital and handled the job."

As Kane continued to explain about the situation at hand, Country kept staring at Giovanni with a puppy dog look on his face. Walking around the table while talking and looking at everyone, Kane noticed the two making goo-goo eyes at each other, but he didn't say anything about it. He just continued talking about what was about to happen next:

"Family, we are 'bout to meet with the two crooked cops. I'm waiting for their phone call so I can find out where to meet them. Other than that, nobody leaves here."

"I have one more thing to speak on. I got a call from my people at the hospital, and she told me that they caught me on tape leaving the hospital. Fam, if anything happens to me or I have to go away for some time, Country will run the house. Don't y'all stop 'cause of me. Y'all keep getting money no matter what."

Kane was interrupted by his phone. He knew it wasn't twelve yet. He didn't recognize the number, but answered it anyway. "Yo, who dis?"

"Kane, this is Angela. I'm calling from a pay phone outside. The police just brought in two dead bodies, and one man that is still alive. They're saying that you killed them too. What's going on, baby?"

"Angela, listen, baby. Ain't no way I could be in two places at once. Those bastards are just trying to put more bodies on me. But to be honest with you, one of my female partners almost got robbed and had to defend herself, and that's the truth. If they're gonna put the bodies on me, they're crazy as hell!"

"Baby, don't worry. Just promise you didn't do it, and I'll take care of the other problem."

"Angela, on my momma and daddy's graves, I didn't

murder them, nor did I have anything to do with it. What are you gonna do?"

"Don't worry. Didn't I say that I love you and would do anything to be with you? Well, let me prove myself, baby. You just take care of yourself and don't get caught up in anymore bullshit. Oh yeah. I knew there was something else I had to tell you. Mrs. Rooney's secretary is the lead agent for the FBI. She's the one that's heading the case against you. Her name is Cindy Palico."

"Cindy is FBI? Baby, I have to call you back. Be careful. I love you, Angela."

Kwantie's eyes grew wide after hearing Kane mention Cindy's name.

Giovanni and Country also heard Cindy's name. Giovanni looked at Country, whose entire facial expression had changed. Looking at Kane, Country knew what was next.

Chapter 32

Hello, is this Kane?"

"Yeah, muthafucker, dis is me. I got da damn money. Where are we gonna make da exchange?"

"We're coming to your turf. We will meet you at the butcher shop. I know you niggers won't try anything stupid at your own place of business. Plus, it sits in the middle of town."

"Cracker, if y'all try any funny shit, I got something for both of y'alls' asses!"

"Anyway, you watermelon, fried chicken eating ass nigger, just have the money right and everything will be all good! We'll see you in a few minutes."

"Kim, remember that envelope I gave you? There are two addresses in it. You and Kwantie each take one and wait on my call. Country, call Shawn and have him come up here right now. We're gonna need all the hands we can get. Everybody else, y'all know y'alls' places."

As Kane was preparing for a small war, he wasn't sure of what the two crooked cops had up their sleeves, but he would be ready for anything.

Kim and Kwantie got up to go their separate ways. Before splitting up, Kim filled Kwantie in on the plans that Kane had given her for this assignment. Kwantie smiled and kissed Kim, and jumped in her car and left.

Kane was getting ready to be the top dawg, and the streets were already trying him. He had promised Country that when this was over with the crooked cops, everybody was going to take a couple of days off.

Interrupted by his cell phone ringing, Kane looked at his caller ID and saw José's number. He hurried up and and answered it.

"Hey, *papi*. My men are in the city. Where do you need them to be?"

"Have them to park outside of the butcher shop I told you about. Is everything still as we planned?"

"Yes. They already know what to do. Call me when it's done. Oh yeah. I almost forgot to tell you that they found my sister, dead. Someone shot her in the chest twice, right there in the hospital. *Gracias, papi!*"

"May I speak to Miss Palico?"

"Hold for a second, please."

"Hello, this is Miss Palico. How may I help you?"

"It's me, baby. It's going down tonight at JB's Butcher Shop. I have to go. I love you!"

Cindy just smiled. Calling an emergency meeting, she filled everybody in on the details and the location.

They didn't have much time, so she had to explain on the way. This was the day that she had been waiting for. This could put her above the rest of her peers. She didn't want any fuck ups.

While speaking over her walkie-talkie, she explained to the other agents what she expected:

"Listen. This crew is dangerous. They are playing for keeps. Word has it that they are connected with one of the major cartels out of Mexico. They are protected by the MS-13's. I want everyone that goes in to come out alive. So keep your heads up and your eyes and ears open. Not one of those people will hesitate to put a bullet in your head. They know how to shoot, so everybody stay on your P's and Q's."

The police department wasn't that far from the butcher shop. They were there and had set up a perimeter in less than fifteen minutes.

While sitting in the van, Cindy was watching as the black Range Rover pulled up. A young kid jumped out and ran into the shop. Ten minutes later, a U-Haul truck pulled into the parking lot at the back of the butcher shop.

Mitch parked the truck right in the middle of the parking lot so that he could watch everything around him. Thomas pulled up in their black Yukon.

Cindy looked through the binoculars and thought she recognized the two white men as they exited their vehicles. Trying to figure out what two white men had to do with Kane and the Mexicans was starting to bother her.

Then, like a bolt of lightning it hit her. She recognized their faces. They were Thomas Howe and his partner, Mitch Crimson—the two agents who had gone undercover at the same time she did. Not understanding what was going on, she radioed for everyone to stand down. She wanted to wait and see how the situation played out.

"Kane, we're outside. Hurry the fuck up with our money. I want to see it first."

"Who do you think you're talking to? Some nickel and dime hustler or a street dummy? Me and my peeps are coming outside, and we want to see Carp. After that, my partner will go back in and get your money."

"Whatever! Just hurry up and bring your ass out here."

Kane looked at Country and gave him a nod.

JB and Shawn headed to the front of the shop and turned the lights off. E-Dubb was standing in the doorway with a Mac-11.

Before stepping out, Country looked back at Giovanni. Winking her eye, she blew him a kiss.

"Where da fuck is Carp at, you pig?"

"Shut the fuck up! He's in the truck. Lift the gate up and show him, partner."

"I hope you ain't playing no games."

When the gate on the back of the truck went up, Kane saw Carp tied to a chair that was sitting in the middle of the truck. Kane yelled his name and asked if he was okay.

After Carp nodded his head, Mitch slammed the gate down and told them to go and get the money.

Kane lifted his hand in the air, and Giovanni stepped out of the door with two black gym bags that were full of money. When she got up to Thomas and Mitch, she stopped and showed them that the bags were full of cash.

Kane looked at the two men and started laughing.

"What the fuck is so funny?"

"You two! You actually thought that you were going to walk away with the money just like that? Are you fucking serious? Before we do anything else, I think you need to talk to someone first, Agents Thomas Howe and Mitch Crimson."

"You think just because you know our names that it's enough to scare us?"

"Well, if that doesn't scare you, what about this?" Kane pulled out his cell phone and dialed seven digits.

When Kim answered, Kane put the speaker phone on so they could hear what was going on. Kim put Thomas's wife on the line. Her screaming made Thomas reach for his gun. But before he could pull it out, Giovanni pulled a pump shotgun from one of the bags of money and aimed it at Thomas and Mitch's chests.

Just to prove that they weren't playing around, Kane hung up the phone and called Mitch's house as well. When Kwantie answered the phone, Mitch heard his wife begging and pleading for her and their kids' lives.

Kane was still laughing.

Shit had hit the fan. There was no way out of this, and Thomas made up his mind that he wasn't going out without a fight.

"Everybody, hold your positions. Wait for my signal. I want to catch them with everything. Did anybody see what was in the U-Haul? Hold on! Hold your positions! There's a car pulling up. It looks like one of ours. I repeat, hold your positions!"

Cindy was watching as the car pulled up with two patrolmen in it. The car pulled around to the back and cut the lights off. The two officers got out and walked up to the truck. They asked everyone what was going on.

Giovanni had turned so the pump shotgun, was hidden by her body.

Cindy noticed that both of the officers were Mexican. "Those are not ours! I repeat, those officers are not ours! Something isn't right! Go! Go! Everybody move in!"

Kane knew what was going on when he saw the police car. He was pretending to be nervous. He told Giovanni to put the shotgun away. But before he could say anything else, the bright light from the Mexican officer's flashlight had blinded everyone.

"Officers, we sure are glad to see you! These people have a man tied up in that truck. I think we stumbled up on a drug deal or a kidnapping gone bad," Kane told them.

Finally, it came to him. Big Country remembered who the white chick in the picture with Giovanni was. "Oh shit, Kane! I knew something wasn't right! This bitch is five-O, dawg! She's an undercover agent! Giovanni is Cindy's partner, Kane! I followed the bitch to her crib, and while I was in there I snatched a picture of her and Cindy!"

Kane didn't hesitate. He knew Country too well to second guess him. Kane instantly reached for his gun, but it was too late.

Giovanni knew she was busted. She didn't even try to explain; she just lifted the shotgun and began to squeeze the trigger. But she was dead before she knew it. Shawn beat her to the draw. He was in the corner of the doorway with a sniper's rifle.

Thomas dove to the ground and got two quick shots off, knocking one of the fake police officers straight off of his feet.

Country and Kane had pulled out their guns and started firing in the direction of the U-Haul truck, trying to hit Thomas before he took cover.

Before they knew it, out of nowhere, police cars and vans pulled up, and S.W.A.T. team members jumped out, screaming. Putting their guns down was out of the question.

E-Dubb came out of the back door letting his Mac-11 rip. He bought enough time for Country to make it to the back door. Kane got stuck on the other side of the parking lot when the police started firing back at E-Dubb and Country.

Once in the butcher shop, JB hit a button on the wall, and the entire floor lifted up to expose an underground getaway. JB went first, leading the way, with Shawn and Country right behind him. E-Dubb brought up the rear with the Mac-11, making sure no one followed them until the floor was closed all the way. Once it had closed, he turned and ran to catch up with the rest of them.

No one was worried about Kane, because they knew that if he got away, he would know where to meet them.

When the real police pulled up, the remaining fake cop turned and ran to his police cruiser. He came out with an AK-47 and tried to take out as many of the real cops as he could. Bodies were falling everywhere when he started chopping away.

None of the other policemen could get a clear shot at him due to his position and angle. But Thomas got a good shot off that caused the fake cop to spin around and drop the assault rifle, after which bullets filled his body from every direction.

When the smoke cleared, Thomas came out from behind the truck with his badge in his hand. He thought he was safe and that it was all over. He looked down at his partner, Mitch and just shook his head.

As all of the agents were putting their guns back into their holsters, a loud boom echoed in the alleyway just as Thomas's head exploded right in front of them.

No one knew where the shots had come from, but Cindy did see Kane take off running down the alley. Wasting no time, she took off right behind him. The other officers tried to keep up with her, but she was running too fast. After turning a couple of corners, they had lost her.

Kane never looked back. Running at top speed, he didn't know that he had turned down a blind alley. After he reached the end of the alley, he heard footsteps getting closer, and he had no choice but to turn and pull his gun out again. He couldn't believe his eyes. Cindy was coming down the alley with her gun drawn.

"Kane, listen, baby. It doesn't have to end this way. I love you. I mean it from the bottom of my heart. I would do anything for you, but I have to take you in alive. I promise that I'll get you off. You will beat every charge the feds bring against you. You have my word."

"Are you crazy? You must think I'm stupid or something! Cindy, this ain't no fucking movie or a book. This shit is real life, not no make believe shit. You are a fucking agent, and that means I'm going to jail or to hell, and I prefer hell any day over jail."

"Listen to me. It doesn't have to be either one. I've

been undercover on this case for a long time. I could have busted you a long time ago, but it's not you we want. We want your connect. Kane, if you just trust me, you won't do any time in jail."

"What are you saying, Cindy? Stop beating around the bush."

"Kane, I know everything. I know the mayor forced you to hustle. I know that Thomas and Mitch were on his payroll. I know they kidnapped Carp, and that he was in the back of the U-Haul. Look, we both lost a lot. I lost Giovanni, who was my partner and my lover, but I'll be damned if I'm going to lose you too. I'm in love with you. Please understand that in order to make this work, I'm going to need you to give me the person at the head of your organization."

"You want me to snitch?"

"Call it what you want to, but all I need is a name and you'll walk away right now like we never had this conversation."

"Are you telling me that if I give you a name right now, you're gonna let me walk away like none of this just happened?"

"Yes, I promise honey."

"Cindy, if you're lying, I promise this won't be over. You're making me go against everything I believe in."

"Look, baby! I'm about to put my gun down. You do the same. All I want is a name so I can replace yours in the paperwork."

Kane knew that he was running out of time and had to make a decision quick. He remembered what José said to him about how nothing is what it seems, and only the dirtiest players survive in this game. But the game had changed, and it wasn't called "snitching" anymore. It was now called "survival".

Kane looked at Cindy and smiled. He leaned forward to kiss her and waited for her to kiss him back. He wanted to make sure that her word was bond. When she kissed him back and placed her tongue in his mouth, it was enough to let him know that she had his back. He stepped back, looked Cindy in the eyes and smiled again before telling her that he loved her too.

Cindy had dropped her guard and relaxed, and waited for him to give her a name. Suddenly, she saw fear in Kane's eyes.

"Big Country, no-o-o-o-o!" Kane yelled out as he began to lift his gun up to shoot.

Two shots were fired, and Cindy fell face down on the ground. As bad as Kane wanted to stay and help her, he knew that he had to run. He never looked back while running down the alley, and leaving her for dead.

Timothy "LYFE" Davis

Dedication

I dedicate this book:

To my parents My Della Burns and Timothy Davis R.I.P.

To my kids Tyra, Timar, Quendarian, Destiny, DeAsha, Angel, Ashanti, Knydren, Timario, and Cody (my grandson)

The road to success is a hard one to travel but at the end of the road is Lyfe's success. Stay focus. My beautiful wife Odessa Davis, Thanks for never giving up on me.

And a special dedication to: The bitter souls and the ones who gave up on me during the struggle, I made it through blood/sweat/and tears.

You can email your comments to him at:
lyfes2ndchance@gmail.com or
timothydavis62@yahoo.com

NEW VISION PUBLICATION

P.O. Box 2815
Stockbridge, GA 30281

Or

P.O. Box 310367
Jamaica, NY 11431

Order Form

Name: ______________________________

Address: ______________________________

City: ____________ State: ________ Zip: ______

Qty.	Title	Price	Total
____	Tit 4 Tat 1	$15.00	______
____	Tit 4 Tat 2	$15.00	______
____	Tit 4 Tat 3	$15.00	______
____	Damaged	$15.00	______
____	Still Damaged	$15.00	______
____	A Blind Shot *(special)*	$8.00	______
____	Boss Lady	$15.00	______
____	Shank	$15.00	______
____	Unfaithful To The Game	$15.00	______
____	The Price of Loyalty	$15.00	______
____	Thicker Than Blood *(special)*	$8.00	______
____	Blood Sweat & Tears	$15.00	______
		Subtotal:	______
		Shipping fees:	______
		Total:	______

Books will be shipped within 7 business days once payment has been processed. All shipments will go out media mail. First book ($3.85); each additional book is $1.50 per book. No personal checks will be accepted. Make institutional checks or money orders payable to: **New Vision Publication** or go to **www.NewvVisionPublication.com** to place an order.